"Where are you?"
Una called to him

Zante came into the room by the connecting door. He wore only a toweling robe and he was as golden, as taut muscled as Apollo.

He crossed the room to stand by the bed looking down at her. Though she was lying down, she hadn't drawn the covers over her. Her arms reached out to him when suddenly, with a flick of the silk sheet, he covered her almost to her chin!

That gesture, as much as the look on Zante's face, warned Una, made her cruelly aware that from lover and mate, he had inexplicably turned enemy.

He was like Othello standing in murderous intent over the wife he found guilty. *But guilty of what,* Una thought frantically. *What have I done?*

OTHER
Harlequin Romances
by JANE ARBOR

The Devil Drives

by

JANE ARBOR

Harlequin Books

TORONTO•LONDON•NEW YORK•AMSTERDAM
SYDNEY•HAMBURG•PARIS•STOCKHOLM

Original hardcover edition published in 1979
by Mills & Boon Limited

ISBN 0-373-02342-1

Harlequin edition published July 1980

CHAPTER ONE

Zante's arm was around Una's shoulders as they stood at the rail of the ferry out from Corfu, now fallen astern as the steamer drew closer to Erikona Island, journey's end.

Zante said, 'Take off your sunglasses, or you'll miss the first and one of the best luxuries of Greece —its incredible light. Too dazzling for you Westerners to bear until you get used to it, but our gift to you of an experience you'll never forget.' Reaching for the shank of her glasses, he removed them for her, dangling them between thumb and forefinger as he watched for her reaction.

Una blinked once, then turned her head slowly, allowing her eyes to feast on the great sweep of sea and sky and a mist of land ahead, of which the details sharpened and coloured as she watched. Blue sea, sky white with heat, green and ochre land, all a-shimmer with a breathtaking incandescence.

'Erikona—*your* island, in *your* light,' she murmured almost reverently, and heard her husband laugh.

'My island, certainly, but God's light. Overstatement gets you nowhere,' he teased her.

'All the same, it must have been the light which made you decide to be a painter,' she retorted.

He shrugged. 'You've got the wrong artist. You're thinking of Canaletto and the light over Venice. I'm only a dilettante who paints when he wants to.'

'Oh, you——! Just because you don't have to paint for your living——!' Una gave in with a laugh and followed the direction of Zante's pointing finger a little to the south.

'Kassikona, Erikona's "baby" there,' he said. 'A rock, a beach, two or three peasants' cabins, a few olives—that's Kassikona, reachable by dinghy in half an hour or so, and the ideal retreat for anyone indulging a fit of the sulks or simply, in a time-worn phrase, wanting to "be alone".'

Una laughed again. 'I'll remember that. I can sail a dinghy,' she hinted demurely.

'Just let me find you trying!' Zante dropped a light kiss on her hair and moved a little way astern, watching the creaming wake. Una turned, supporting herself by her spread arms on the rail and studied him.

Her handsome husband! Her *classically* perfect-of-face-and-stature husband! Eyes the blue of dark sapphires under their hooding of blue-veined lids; gold-brown hair sweeping back from sculpted profile, brows and nose in as straight a line as that of a head on a Greek fresco; height and sun-bronzed body eloquent of the supple strength of an Apollo, an Achilles, a Perseus ... In the sheer beauty of his virility Zante Diomed matched them all.

And, miracle of miracles! his wooing and his kisses claimed to love *her*! No miracle at all that she should have fallen to *his* magnetism, for how many girls and women must have done so before her? Yet it was she to whom he had laid determined siege and had married. And which of her vulnerable sex, with no serious love-affair in her present or her past, would not have been at first flattered, then willingly drawn to him, then have fallen headlong in love with him, as she had?

His smile had a special magic for her. His withdrawal to gravity after it was like a clouding of the sun—a temporary clouding only, for so far she had never seen him angry, though there was a lift to his chin and a firm set to his jawline which advised that, given occasion, he could be. If it ever happened and she were involved in such an occasion, she sensed she must fear it. And once her father, understandably concerned by their whirlwind courtship, had said of Zante's smile, 'It's a shade ambiguous——' and then had corrected himself to—'No, that sounds two-faced, which I'm sure he isn't. Enigmatic was the word I really wanted—as if he's thinking more than his expression is saying,' a judgment on the smile she loved which Una had laughingly dismissed as 'snap' and unworthy of her father's genuine liking and respect for Zante.

'And you do, in your heart, believe I can be happy with him?' she had appealed. In answer to which Daniel Keith had reassured her,

'Yes, darling, I do hope and believe I can trust you to him—just as I'm equally sure you're going to do your loyal, loving best with him.' And with that accolade of Daniel's faith in her and in her husband-to-be, Una had been very, very content.

Zante was beckoning to her now and she went to him.

'Look,' he said, pointing down at a big plate-shape rolling lazily in the water in the wake of the steamer. 'It's a turtle,' he said. 'Have you ever seen one in the flesh and the shell before?'

'Only in an aquarium,' she said, peering and admiring the greys and greens and browns of the great carapace. It followed the ship until the sudden churning and wash of the propellers warned of the entry into harbour, when, alarmed, it turned and swam seaward, out of sight.

Now it was possible to discern small shops and warehouses and a couple of taverns on the quay. Narrow canyons of streets ran back from it and behind it a road climbed, necklace-wise, up scrub and olive-covered slopes. Near the top was a glimpse of white among the trees. 'Your future home. *To Aspro Spiti*—The White House,' Zante told Una, who turned her binoculars on it eagerly, the Greek island home of a girl named Una Diomed who, only as late as yesterday morning, had still been Una Keith, spinster of Sutton parish in the university city of Falconbridge, England; who had been transported by night to this enchantment of scene and prospect —it had almost to be a dream! But it wasn't. It was happening to her. It was real.

As, though equally incredibly, were the six weeks which had passed since the Vice-Chancellor's dinner-party to which she and her father, by virtue of his professorship in archaeology, had been invited. Mrs Vice-Chancellor—she had a name, though out of her hearing, few people used it—collected 'lions' as others collect stamps or antiques, and her guest of the evening that night had been Zante Diomed, the Greek painter, fresh from a nonchalant showing of his work in London. And from there everything had begun to happen.

The talk at the dinner-table had been fairly general, but that between Zante and the Professor had been of the latter's recent fieldwork, tracing the extent of Greek trade with Egypt in the sixth and seventh centuries, and of his plans now to seek in Greece and some of its satellite islands, clues to a reciprocal trade in the opposite direction.

'We know, you see,' Una had heard Daniel telling Zante, 'that Greece sold to Egypt pottery and silver and olive oil. Ships and mercenary soldiers too. And that Greece received in return grain and Egyptian jewellery and alabaster and architectural ideas. But we are always looking for more evidence of the extent of the distribution of the goods. Which makes fieldwork in Greece the next project I'm hoping to undertake, though privately this time. In Egypt I was commissioned for work sponsored by the Museum.'

Later, tête-à-tête with Una, Zante had questioned her part in her father's work. She had found it astonishingly easy to talk to his genuine interest. 'I'm sort of a general assistant,' she had told him. 'I'm one of the first on any site. I take notes and measurements; I photograph; I pay wages and chivvy the voluntary helpers. Later, when the finds come in, I bag-up and label and record every day's

loot, and then turn secretary to take dictation of my
father's papers on the work.'

'In other words, you work something like a
twelve-hour day?' Zante had asked in his attractively
accented but colloquially perfect English.

She had smiled, 'More than that, sometimes.'

'You were in Egypt with him?'

'Yes. We came back about nine months ago.'

'And since?'

'Father has been lecturing at the University. I've
been keeping house for him, and still playing secretary.'

'But with time, one hopes, for boy-friends and
fun?'

'Some,' she had admitted, without going into details of how ephemeral student relationships tended
to be, or of how heartwhole and detached she cur-
rently was.

It was a state of mind and heart and body which
hadn't lasted. A few days later Zante had sought out
the Professor to suggest that he survey a site on the
island of Erikona, Zante's home and in his private
possession. Local tradition had it that it was rich in
archaeological specimens, though within Zante's
memory, it had not been excavated seriously. The
Professor had accepted the offer eagerly, and from
then on Zante had set himself determinedly to Una's
pursuit.

And then, a week ago—— She would marry him
and go out to Erikona as his wife? And the Professor
would go out with them too? To which question

Una had rapturously answered Yes, though her father had demurred with a No. He had no wish, he had told Zante wryly, to emulate the mother in the song who 'came too' on her daughter's honeymoon. So he would travel out to Erikona a day or two behind them, and what was more, since he was an early-to-bed and early-to-rise man and liked his evenings to himself, he would lodge at a handy *taverna* if Zante would find one for him.

There was a friendly informality about the docking of the steamer, with passengers and crew exchanging pleasantries and enquiries for the health of relatives before they parted. 'Most of them have been on day trips or to market in Corfu,' Zante explained to Una as, with only one or two other people, they waited on the quay for their heavy luggage to be offloaded. Zante phoned for his handyman-gardener to bring down the car, and when it arrived he took the wheel himself for the drive up to the house.

The narrow road, white with dust, ran between low loose-stone walls and much use of the horn was necessary at its climbing hairpin turns. It had levelled out before Zante turned in at a pair of high scrolled iron gates and drew up before the house which he had pointed out from the harbour.

It was certainly of a dazzling whiteness, each of its windows offset by shutters of an equally vivid blue. Its frontage was a colonnade of round arches affording shade to the ground floor rooms and the wide main doorway. A massive courtyard gate flanked the building at one end; at the other, another wrought-iron gate gave a glimpse of colour and gardens behind it.

Una gasped. 'Well?' Zante asked, his hands still on the steering-wheel while the man, Giorgio, took off the luggage.

'It's so—so utterly picture-postcard Greek!' she breathed.

'But not too Greek, one hopes, to make you homesick for a Falconbridge suburb?'

Beneath her lashes she threw him a look that was full of love. 'Homesick—for *anywhere*—with you?' she murmured, and was rewarded by his quick squeeze of her hand before he alighted and helped her out.

She had been painfully shy of this moment—coming 'home' with Zante, his bride of a day, though, through the timing of their journey, not yet his wife. Zante hadn't seemed to want to linger in England for even one night of honeymoon, and she had been happy about that. But with the prospect of his claiming her only a few hours ahead now, she had been stricken with panic—half delicious, half fearful—as soon as her feet had touched Erikona's Greek soil.

Supposing ... supposing he was disappointed in her?

Supposing their kisses, at first tentative, then increasingly passionate with promise, were to be followed by an anti-climax of reality? Supposing their controlled but compulsive awareness of each other's bodies hadn't the ecstatic power to toss them to the heights which they hoped? She *loved* Zante—in every way of which her body and spirit sang. But would her need *of* him, her response *to* him tell him all he wanted to know, tell him all that she had to give?

At this point of her homecoming with him, there were other more mundane problems too; learning the ways of his household, its personnel and the new language in which she would have ultimately to address them. Zante said that, since the tourist boom, most Greeks had at least a smattering of English-American and would smile their congratulations on every Greek word she managed to utter. But she was going to feel alien and dumb and deaf, all the same.

And there was also Madame Maria Diomed, Zante's widowed aunt by marriage, who made her home with him. Having been to school in England, she spoke English fluently, Zante had told Una. But she was a partial invalid, suffering prolonged and violent attacks of migraine which prostrated her, forcing her to keep to her room, sometimes for days at a time. She had her own maid-cum-nurse and took little part in the running of the house, so wouldn't interfere with Una's taking of the reins, Zante said. 'She is not a very happy person, you'll find. But she has cause, and you must learn to accept her, as she will accept you.'

'Have you any cousins by her?' Una had asked, and he had said No. Nor had he sisters nor brothers, nor parents now. They had been caught in their car in an ambush during the troubles in Cyprus, leaving him, Zante, heir to Erikona, in his family's possession through countless long centuries. He farmed vines and olives for the islanders' benefit, and painted for his own satisfaction. That he was rich by his work was neither here nor there. He had a compulsion to paint which he indulged. It was as simple as that.

From Giorgio Zante had learned that his aunt was not likely to appear to welcome them, so, directing the man to put their bags in the hall, Zante threw open the big door himself, ushering Una inside.

For a split second she had hesitated on the threshold, shyly and foolishly hoping ... But when Zante gave no sign of being aware of any omission on his part, she decided that, being Greek, he might never have heard of a certain silly English marriage custom. Or did he know of it, and meant to carry her over the threshold of their bridal room tonight ... ? Thrilling to the thought, she went to join him in the hall.

People appeared—two bobbing, smiling maids, a mature and buxom cook, and a girl in a nurse's apron whom Zante took aside and questioned briefly after he had introduced her to Una as Beria, his aunt's nurse-companion. As Giorgio had suggested, Aunt Maria was not well enough to come down, Una learned; Zante did not mean to disturb her.

He showed Una the main downstair rooms while one of the girls went ahead with her hand luggage. There was an elegant salon, a dining-room and another room, the fourth wall of which consisted of sliding glass doors giving on to the gardens, a veritable suntrap.

'Where do you paint?' she asked.

'I have a studio opening off my bedroom. But mostly I work on my actual scene. I even sometimes camp out overnight if, for instance, I want to capture the effect of a particular moment of light on a landscape,' said Zante.

'Oh! And will you give me due notice when you're going to do that?' she challenged him lightly.

'Would you rather I'd said that, as a bachelor, I used to do it?'

'Not at all, as long as you'll let me go with you!'

'And supposing I were ungallant enough to tell you that you wouldn't be welcome?' he teased.

'You daren't. I should go all the same!'

The fine polished staircase, balustered by wrought-iron, gave on to a first floor, equally airy and spacious. Zante pointed out his aunt's suite, then opened the door to a room so big and so dominated by a richly carved huge fourposter that Una took a step backward in awe of it.

'The bride's suite,' Zante stood aside to allow her to enter. He nodded to one end of the room. 'You've your private shower and closets adjoining—there.'

She was still staring at the bed. 'I've never slept in anything of that size!' she marvelled.

'It was my parents' room and the bed is an heirloom, designed for just such an occasion as this.'

'And—you?' He had said 'your' shower and 'my

bedroom'. He must have meant his dressing-room, she decided. For surely he couldn't mean to consign her to this—this *acreage* of room and bed space alone?

'I?' He answered her hesitant question with another nod at the other end of the room. 'Next door. Come and see,' he invited.

She went with him through a connecting door into a much smaller room, austere and masculine in contrast to the curtaining and furnishings of the other. There was a made-up bed in it, so it wasn't merely a dressing-room, but suddenly Una was able to laugh inwardly at her misgivings.

Of course, if it was where he always slept, newly returned to the house, he would still call it his bedroom by habit! *They* would occupy 'the bridal suite' from now on. *They* would be together ...

The room to which a further door stood open— his studio—was glaringly light by reason of a glass-panelled ceiling. Its floor was bare, its furnishing functional—a long wooden table, a wall cupboard, a couple of easels and a low dais with a chair.

Una pointed to the dais. 'For your models?' she asked.

He threw her a sideways glance. 'Jealous?'

'Yes. Madly!'

'As you know very well, I don't paint portraits,' he said.

He left her to unpack and freshen and change her dress, and when she joined him he ordered tea, fragrant with lemon, and little almond cakes to be served to them in the sun-room. He already had plans for their evening. He hadn't yet organised any rooms for the Professor, so he would do that, charter a hire-car to run him to and from the site when he began to work on it, and then they would dine at a *taverna* where Una must sample Greek food and drink for the first time. During their brief courtship he had sometimes taken her out to Greek restaurant meals. But now she must be educated in the real thing.

Una would have preferred to spend their first evening at home. In fact, she had wondered whether his aunt's absenting of herself might be part tact, as well as a crippling migraine, to allow them to be alone together. But even her short knowledge of Zante had taught her that when he made a plan he liked to carry it out, and she was willing to go along with that.

After tea he showed her the gardens, a wonder of flower and shrub growth on what must be an arid, sun-baked soil. In that month of March the spring flowers and the almond blossom were already over and the summer lilies and orange trees were blooming long before their English time. The sun sank in a cloudless lemon sky, and the air, even at dusk, was as lightly warm as a silk cloak.

The inn which Zante had in mind for the Professor's stay was near to the harbour, and his rather starkly furnished rooms had a view of it. Zante introduced the proprietor and his beaming wife to Una, and suggested they dine there on the acacia-shaded terrace by candlelight and to the whisper and lap-lap of the sea on the harbour walls.

By Greek custom, they were invited into the kitchens to choose their meal. Una rejected the highly recommended octopus with a little shiver of distaste. She settled instead for a more recognisable *pilaff* of shrimps, followed by a pie of meat and vegetables called *moussaka*. Dessert was fresh fruit and the inevitable *baklava* cakes, honey-sweet and melting, and they drank *etalya*, a dry white wine. It was all very leisurely and rather alien, and the sweetest memory Una was to carry away from that evening was of the moment when Zante stood, held out his hand to her, and said, 'Let's go home.'

The white house was luminous in the moonlight. It was late, and inside all was quiet, but a tray of drinks had been left in the hall. Zante poured for himself, but Una declined. He said, 'I'll be with you in as little time as you need. How long?'

She mentally waved goodbye to the bride-over-the-threshold bit. He couldn't know of it, but she promised herself she would tease him about the omission at a less electric moment than this. 'A quarter of an hour?' she offered, and went alone up the stairs when he nodded.

Later she was to wonder at what moment—if there had been one—she might have admitted to a flicker of disappointment with this wedding evening. And if there had been, she was to reflect, it would have been this one when, with nothing and nobody to delay them, they did not go up to their rooms together. But at the time her only thought of Zante was a wry, 'At this point, I believe he's as shy as I am. Perhaps men *are*!'

The big room, softly lighted, was waiting for her. With the drawing of the curtains and the unpacking of her heavier luggage, the luxurious bed had been turned down. She stood in fascinated contemplation of it for some time before she began to undress. At last she dropped the filmy chiffon of her trousseau nightgown over her head, shook its folds to floor-level and saw herself, bridal and expectant, in three mirrors at once. Did she really *deserve* Zante's loving and marrying her? *Did she?*

She heard him come up and go to his room by its door into the corridor. How and where would she wait for him to come to her? Sitting on her dressing-stool? In bed? Yes, that was it. When he came in, she would open her arms wide to him, draw him down to her ... need him ... love him—as hungry for him as he would be for her.

He came in by the connecting door. He wore only a knee-length towelling robe, her golden-bodied, taut-muscled Apollo! If her fingers could think, they would be longing to trace the hard line of shoulder-bone to neck-hollow and down the braced chest to waist and thigh. His body would be hard and urgent with desire for her, and they would both *know*—

He crossed the room to stand by the bed, looking down at her. Though she was lying down, she hadn't drawn anything over her. Her arms were ready for him, but they didn't open to him when, with a flick at the silk sheet and coverlet, he covered her almost to her chin. And it was in that gesture—in any other context, a solicitous, caring one—as much as from the look on his face, that she was warned, made cruelly aware that from lover and mate-to-be, he had suddenly turned enemy. He was an Othello, standing in murderous intent over Desdemona. And, like Desdemona, *she did not know why*.

Her heart began to beat hammer-blows against her ribs. She thrust herself up against her pillows where, more level with him, she felt a little less at the mercy of that pitiless downward gaze. Physical murder couldn't be in his heart. But judgment and rejection of her could, and his expression was so eloquent of both that she hardly managed to question tremulously, 'You ... don't ... want me?'

She got no answer. Instead he said, 'I hope you're comfortable; that you have everything you need. Meanwhile, the best thing I can wish you is that you sleep well.' He paused. 'As well, that is, as your conscience may let you. Goodnight.'

'My *conscience*?' As he turned away, she caught at his hand. 'Zante, why? What have I done? Something wrong to you? How? When?' she pleaded.

With an easy turn of his wrist he freed his hand. 'You could try examining your conscience as the prayer-book advises. As far as I'm concerned, you'll have time enough—except when I may choose that you apply your faculties differently.' He was crossing the floor now. 'When you wake in the morning, ring for a maid to bring you coffee, or whatever you want. I shall sleep in my own room, but if you are going to suffer from bridal pride in front of the domestics, I'm quite willing to visit you for the few minutes it would take me to ruffle the other side of your bed.' His door to his bedroom closed behind him with a soft whisper that, to Una's ears, was as dismissing and insolent as any deafening slam.

When he had gone, she crept out of bed, moved over to her dressing-table and confronted her image in its mirror.

Shoulder-length dark hair coaxed under at the tips; in certain lights with a raven-blue sheen to it. Grey eyes under level brows; forehead which should have been higher for beauty; straight, finely nostriled nose; pale skin; unremarkable chin and jawline; a profile which only the long column of neck and throat could lift out of the ordinary. Figure? No more than the long-legged slenderness which dozens of girls of her age could claim—that was Una Diomed, née Una Keith, twenty-four years of age, serious, reserved, with no claim to 'zing' or sex-appeal—the Una Keith who had deluded herself she had been wooed and married for love, instead of caught and trapped by a sadism she had allowed to ensnare her because, fool that she had been, she had wanted it to ensnare her!

She was too shocked to cry; too stingingly aware of Zante's injustice to indulge any sentimental mourning for the fiasco of her wedding night. He had made it clear that he hadn't left her at some warped but passing whim, but was punishing her at the dictate of a measured judgment of some imaginary wrong she had done him. He had planned this *before* he had married her; he had married her *because* his rejection of her was a revenge he had meant all along to wreak!

Convinced of that, she took some time to call up the courage to confront him with a demand that he tell her the truth. Then, just as she was, in filmy nightgown and barefoot, she went to his door, knocked at it, and without waiting for his permission walked into his room.

He was sitting with his back to her, writing at an antique bureau. He turned, pen in hand, and gestured her to a chair.

'If you've come for a showdown which you aren't going to enjoy, you'd better sit down,' he said, then swivelled right round to face her at a distance of several yards. 'Well?' he invited coldly, his face as dark with anger and contempt as when he had stood at her bedside. Seeing it, she realised there was nothing to be gained by appealing to him, so she fell back upon accusation.

She sat down with her hands clasped between her knees to hide their trembling. 'You are my husband,' she stated. 'You made love to me. You've married me——'

'Did I have to drag you by your hair to the altar?'

She flinched. 'No. Because I made it so clear that I loved you, it must have been easy.'

'I had to work at it. But yes—easy enough for my purpose,' he shrugged.

'And your purpose was——?' When he did not reply, she answered her question herself. 'It was to marry me, pretending you loved me, and then to cheat me in the only way you guessed would matter to me. But why?'

'Are you claiming your conjugal rights, as I believe they are called?'

At that her rising anger almost exploded. 'If I were fool enough to claim anything from you, obviously I'd be wasting my time,' she raged. 'No, all I can hope for is a grain of the common justice which wouldn't deny to even a criminal the reason for his charge!'

'And in your own eyes, you're no criminal?'

'Well, am I?' she challenged

'In the strictest sense, no,' he allowed. 'Morally——'

'*Morally!* What do you mean?'

He shook his head slowly, as if in despair of the failings of an imbecile. 'No clues? No guilty memory?' He paused, eyebrows lifted in query. 'The name Jason Mithredes—conveniently forgotten, meaning nothing to you now?'

Una stared at him, wide-eyed. 'Jason ... Mithredes?' she echoed slowly. 'Y-e-s——'

'Whom you drove to his death?'

'*Whom I——?*' The silence which followed her horrified, broken question was almost a tangible thing. And Zante allowed it to go on, to stretch out, using it as a weapon against her bewilderment and baffled defeat.

CHAPTER TWO

THE accusation was so monstrous that, on any other lips than Zante's, Una could almost have dismissed it with a scornful laugh.

Jason Mithredes. The young Greek ex-student who had been on the archaeological expedition to Egypt, but who had been recalled by the Museum under a shadow and liable to prosecution for theft —of course she remembered him. She had had to play a part in his apprehension, but later, when he had had a fatal accident in his car while he was on bail, she had not even been in England herself. So how could Zante——? How dared he?

She realised he was watching her with almost a feline predator's unblinking stare ... waiting. She forced herself to enough calm to say, 'Yes, I did know a young man of that name last year, and I know he's dead now. But I had no part in that. And what was he to you?'

'He was my cousin by marriage.'

'You told me you had none!' Una contradicted.

'You asked me whether my Aunt Maria had any children who would be my cousins. And she hasn't. Has she—thanks to you?' he accused.

Una worked it out. 'But her name—the same as yours, you said. And his—Mithrèdes. How?'

'Jason was her son by her first mariage. Her marriage to my uncle was her second.'

'Which made Jason no real relation to you,' Una argued logically, only to evoke Zante's guttural, 'Ach! Split hairs, would you? He was my mother's sister's son, and close enough for my family's blood to demand vengeance for his death!'

Una stared at him, as at a stranger. Gone was her lover. Gone her husband. Gone her hope of a happy, romantic marriage. Angry, incredulous, 'And you've planned to take out that revenge on *me* for no reason at all!' she scorned.

'With cause, I think.'

'With *no* cause! I hardly knew your cousin. He was a student at the University and he came to my father's lectures on ancient history. He dropped out before taking a degree, but he got a job with the Museum that sponsored the dig in Egypt last year——'

Zante moved impatiently. 'Yes, of course I know all that.'

'And that out there he was guilty of the theft of a priceless Clazomenian black-figure vase which he planned to sell to contacts he had in Cairo?'

'I know he was accused of it.'

'He was *guilty* of it,' she insisted. 'When they searched his lodgings, they found stolen seals and coins too.'

'A search which was set up on your evidence against him, I understand?'

She inclined her head. 'Evidence I would have been sub-poenaed to give. I knew he had stolen the vase; that he had broken into the safe where it had been left for one night before shipping. I also knew he badly needed money, for he had asked me to lend him some.'

'Which virtuously you refused to do?'

'I hadn't it to lend, or I'd have tried to help him.'

'But instead "helped" him to prosecution and later to his suicide by adding your damning piece to whatever case the Museum had against him?'

'I had to tell what I knew. Besides, though he might have got rid of the small things, he hadn't a hope of selling the vase. No fence would have dared to try and sell it to a museum or a collector; it simply hadn't a price, as he should have known, but didn't. And then, when he had been recalled and charged, my father had a heart attack—his second— and we were in Egypt until he was convalescent.' Una's chin lifted suddenly. 'You said "suicide"?' she echoed in horror. 'You accuse me of having driven Jason to *suicide*? He had an accident in his car before the case came to court; he drove into the river!'

'On a fine night, no other vehicle involved? I was at the inquest. Were you?'

'No. Father and I were still abroad. But we heard the verdict was accidental death!'

'A charitable reading of the facts which it was hard to understand. The car was dredged up and showed no reason for its failure to keep on the road.'

'But as his theft was his first offence, it was bound to be dealt with leniently.'

'He couldn't know that. And something you wouldn't understand—he was probably obsessed by the disgrace for his family if he were brought to court.'

'What about the disgrace and sorrow for his mother from his suicide?'

Zante shook his head. 'Potential suicides don't think rationally, weighing this against that. No, my dear, wriggle as you may, you bought what was coming to you when you could have held your tongue from accusing him, and didn't.'

'Don't call me your "dear", when I'm not and never have been!' Una flared. 'And mine wasn't the only evidence against him. I could have lied or said nothing, and the Museum would still have prosecuted him. They were determined to make him an example.'

'Still wriggling?' Zante insinuated. 'Suggesting that I should have married the Museum for my family's honour's sake, instead of you?'

'Your family honour!' she scorned. 'Just how is it served by lying and cheating and trapping me into a marriage which you never intended should mean anything—real? Well, *something* seems to have escaped you in all your plotting, Zante Diomed! Namely, that there's a legal answer to a marriage of this sort—it can be annulled!'

'Annulled? Oh no, I think not. Not this one,' said Zante very quietly.

'What do you mean—not this one? It won't have been——'

Equally quietly, 'Consummated is the word you want,' he cut in. 'But at the merest hint you were making that your plea, be very sure, my virgin wife, that I could make it an untenable stand any time I chose.'

Una gasped. 'That—that would be rape!'

'Not as the law rules in Greece, and I believe in England too. Besides, on the evidence of our courting days, I'm inclined to think I mightn't have to force you. I could probably have taken you already in certain of your softened moods, had I cared to try.'

Shamed and outraged to her core, she retorted, 'That was when I loved you and thought you loved me. You've destroyed all that. Now I dare you to touch me—in that way—again. If you ever did, it would be for the last and only time.'

'That sounds like a threat.'

'It was meant as one!'

'Though you shouldn't be too sure of carrying it out. Bodies are notorious for betraying their owners' wills. Or is that too crude a truth for you to accept?'

She ignored the question and went on, 'And aren't you going to—I was going to say "suffer", but "incommoded" would probably be a better word—— Isn't it going to incommode you, by having married someone you hate but won't release?'

He appeared to agree. 'It's a thought,' he allowed. 'And if it gives you any satisfaction, you're welcome to it. But I'd remind you I'm a man, and——'

'And because women are easy, you aren't going to be inconvenienced at all!' she finished for him.

'Now it's you who are being crude,' he reproved, 'but I'm glad you take my point—namely that, though celibacy doesn't bother me at the moment, I can take steps to deal with it, if or when it does.'

'And what about me—if or when enforced celibacy didn't suit *me*?' she flashed.

'That it shouldn't suit you, that you should suffer it on my terms was why I married you,' he pointed out cruelly. 'You've a moral guilt to expiate, and if you try to escape by the door of promiscuity, you'll enjoy the consequences even less. Meanwhile there are other reasons why you won't attempt the way of annulment either. There's your father, for one.'

'Father? How does he——?'

'Come into it? Because he likes and approves of me; he is happy about our marriage; through me, he is looking forward to months of the work that he loves. He has had—hasn't he?—two bad heart attacks already. So what do you suppose it would do to him to learn that he had given you in no-marriage to a monster, and that you could only be freed—if you could—through the publicity of an annulment case? For there would be publicity, I'm afraid. I'm something of a well-known type in society in both England and Greece, and a defended case between you and me would have enormous news value——'

'Following a kind of King Cophetua and the beggar-maid situation, I suppose?' Una sneered.

His smile was a mere lift to his mouth, without mirth. 'Not quite,' he said. 'I believe Cophetua married the girl for the best and most usual of motives—because he fell in love with her.'

'In other words, there's no parallel between him and you?'

Zante shrugged. 'You put things so pithily,' he said, making the irony hurt before he went on. 'As I was saying, there would considerably more news value to our story than the university circles of Falconbridge would care for. Hence, probably some ostracism of the Professor. Had you thought of that?'

'I don't have to think about it. Father will stand by me, once he learns the truth.'

'But he is not going to hear it. I forbid it.'

'*You* forbid it!'

'For his sake. For his work's sake. The shock of the truth could well prove too much for him so soon upon our marriage, so whether or not you agree, as far as he is concerned, we are to appear the happily matched couple of his hopes for us. Likewise, my aunt must know nothing either.'

'You mean she hasn't been a party to your revenge on me?'

'No, that's a responsibility I took upon myself. She is soured enough already over the needless loss of her son, and I have kept my near-certainty of it from her, knowing what further embitterment might do to her—and to her acceptance of you.'

'You actually considered *me*?'

'Deeply, I assure you,' he nodded. 'Maria Diomed has all the traditional fire and passion of our Greek women, and if she suspected your part in Jason's death, I'd hardly care to answer for the conquences. As it is, you'll find her moody depression quite enough to deal with as a day-to-day cross, as well as your disappointment in—shall we call them? —matters marital.'

Almost between her teeth Una ground out, 'You used the right word of yourself—you *are* a monster!'

'Merely, my dear, a man with a strong sense of family duty and a determination that his revenge shall be sweet,' Zante corrected blandly.

'I'd say,' she retorted, 'you're suffering from over-inflated ideas of what any man has the right to take upon himself, not to speak of his hope of success. Supposing I refuse to take either your rejection of our marriage or your aunt's character failings, what then?'

'Character failings—a widow's mourning of her only son? I'm afraid you're going to have to show her more charity than that. And I think you will take the situation as it stands. For the reason of your father.'

'Are you daring me to take it?'

'Are you daring me to force you to take it?' He stood and came over to where she sat. His hands took her roughly by the shoulders and there was a warning fire in his eyes as he looked down at her.

He said darkly, 'I should hate to use physical violence on you at this stage. But I could. Crucify your father; endanger Aunt Maria's sanity, and you could learn just what justified enmity could mean, my girl!'

She was impotent beneath his hold, but he released her and stood back. 'Now,' he said, 'we'll have no more of "taking" or "not taking". Nor of an annulment case within a week of marriage. It wouldn't hold water, you know, nor be worth all the alarums and excursions and the distress. And if you'd thoughts of bringing it later, as I've said, by then I could well have decided to furnish irrefutable evidence against—— And so, tomorrow we shall go together to meet the steamer bringing the Professor from Corfu, smiling our honeymoon smiles and holding our peace.' He held out his hand to her. 'Come, it's time you were in bed. I'll see you to it.'

Una stood up. 'Thank you, but I'll go alone— tonight, as on every other night I spend in this hateful house,' she said.

He turned away. 'As you please. But don't blame the house. There's room enough in it for us not to touch, except before our public. Unless, that is, you'd care to take up my offer to rumple your bed every morning?'

She ignored the gibe and went through to her room, slamming the connecting door behind her. She went over to the bed, sank on her knees beside it, buried her head on her arms and let the angry, agonised tears come. They were the physical reaction to her shock, and while they flowed she was scarcely capable of thought. But when at last she crept into bed and her body curled into a defensive huddle, no sleep came in a merciful blunting of her mind.

She felt as if a beloved, trusted animal had suddenly turned and savaged her, red-eyed in its ferocity, without reason. And Zante's betrayal was worse, far worse. For his had been no unthinking, instinctive attack. It had been calculated with cunning and timed with cruel expertise. A pointer to that had been his reluctance to spend their first night of marriage in England. He had meant that she should experience and be thrilled by the promise of their fulfilment in this lovely world of his island home, only to snatch away the core of it—his pseudo-love—at the very moment which every woman must fear and long for in the maze of emotion that was bridehood.

He must have known that she had fallen in love with him. Since their first week of courting, she had never made any secret of his being her idol and her ideal, so that he had been able to work on that, as well as on her care for her father—knowing that for all her defiance of him, both loves would prove too much for her physical escape from him.

For one betrayal did not kill love, and he would be shrewd enough to realise she would be captive to him until love died at the instance of some even greater injury he might do her in the future. He knew she would stay; that she would show a fair, happy face to the world; that she would spare her father the truth; that, even if fate offered her a chance, she would not take a lover. He might even have guessed how nearly she had betrayed her self-respect to him tonight when briefly he had offered her his hand, saying 'Come.'

For nearly, so very nearly then, she had abjectly reached for it and clung to it; beseeched and pleaded her innocence in vain and put herself still further in his power. Only a vestige of pride had had saved her.

Yet she had *longed* to admit his power with her.

She had always thought of it as the lodestar of their
marriage which would make it work. The ache to
know that she could look to him, lean upon him,
was scarcely less than the yearning ache of her body
for his—a pain that wasn't going to be assuaged.

She must have slept towards morning, for she wasn't
aware when the sun had begun to bar the carpet
with light from between the louvred shutters. Fully
awake to facing a day which she dreaded, she got out
of bed and went to open the shutters on to a reful-
gence which was dazzling even at an hour when
nothing in house or garden seemed to be astir,
though someone must have been, for a whirling-
spray hose-stand was spattering lawns and flower-
beds with a fine arching mist.

Standing at the window, she thought, If she were
going to escape, this would be the time to go—
if Zante's diabolic timing hadn't brought her to an
island from which the only way of departure was
by water. The Corfu steamer called only when it
had passengers to pick up or set down; Zante owned
a motor-launch, and there was the dinghy which—
only happy yesterday!—he had playfully dared her
to use alone.

But the lack of escape route did not matter very
much. For with the daylight her resolution was
hardening; she was not going to run away. Putting
distance between herself and Zante at this stage
would do nothing for her plight. For as he had
taunted her in another connection, she had
'bought' this trauma by having loved him too will-

ingly, too early, and if she had to pay for that by playing the part he had allotted to her, she would until—— But beyond that 'until' was unknown country.

Until Zante was to be convinced Jason's death had not been suicide? Until her love for him died? Until some feeling for her was born in him? Until they failed to convince either her father or Maria Diomed that all was not well with their marriage? How could she know? The future was without a key.

She went through to the luxuriously scented bathroom and she was sitting at her dressing-table, brushing her hair, when there was a scrabble of fingertips at the door to the corridor and Zante came in. He was fully dressed in shirt and pale beige slacks and sandals.

She put down her brush and turned, a hand going defensively to each of her bare upper arms. But he scarcely glanced at her as he went to sit on the far side of her bed.

'You are dressing,' he said. 'Why didn't you ring for early tea—or coffee, if you prefer it?'

'I woke early, and I didn't know what the household routine was,' she replied.

'The "routine", as you call it, is just what you choose to make it,' he returned brusquely. 'The servants are there to obey you. My own programme when I'm here is usually that I get up early and go out, and have breakfast on the patio when I come back.'

'Was it you who turned on the sprinkler in the garden?'

'Yes. Did I disturb you when I left my room?'

'No. And could we do that—have breakfast together on the patio?'

'Meaning that you see the prudence of accepting our relationship as I outlined it last night?'

She forced herself to turn back to her dressing-table and to continue brushing her hair. 'Meaning that you seem to have given me no choice—for the moment,' she said over her shoulder.

'For more than a moment, I hope, for your father's sake and for your own, if you should give my aunt cause to suspect your hand in Jason's death.'

'If you had ever cared to shield me from her blame, you shouldn't have put me in the way of it, by bringing me into her orbit,' Una retorted to his reflection in her mirror.

'And cheated myself of administering the justice that I considered you deserved?' Zante shook his head. 'No, my dear, my *not* marrying you would have asked too much of my tolerance of your guilt.'

'In other words, luring me into marriage you saw as your major punishment of me?'

'Not, as I've mentioned, that you were over-reluctant to be lured,' he commented. 'But yes, a term of marriage which you wouldn't enjoy did seem to be, shall we say, a condign penalty to ask of you.' He paused. 'And as, for your own reasons, you appear to realise the sense of accepting my terms—yes, I agree, breakfast together on the patio could be a pleasant overture to our day.'

Without replying, Una stood and went to pick up the low-cut sun-dress which she had thrown across the bed. But Zante was before her in taking it up. He examined it, found that it went on like a coat and held it open for her. She backed up to him, poignantly aware of his nearness, a-quiver to turn and throw herself into his arms, and when, after slipping the dress on to her shoulders, his hands lingered there for an unnecessary moment or two, she thought in pain, *This is how it would be if he really loved me—the merest touch of flesh, and we should both be on fire.* But as it was, she suspected him of a refinement of torture of her; he knew his effect upon her only too well, and was going to take pleasure in exploiting it.

In order to hide her chagrin from him, she bent and made an awkwardness over fastening the single waist-button of the dress, whose brief wrap-over skirt was fully revealing of her slender legs and thighs. She strapped her bare feet into sandals, straightened and said in a small taut voice, 'I'm ready.'

They walked downstairs together.

As it happened, however, they were to be spared the ordeal of a make-believe honeymoon breakfast, for Maria Diomed was at the patio table ahead of them. Una took swift, anxious measure of her before Zante introduced them.

Zante had said she was in her middle fifties, but she looked much older, and leaning against her chair was the kind of crutch associated with a grand-motherly woman—an ebony, silver-topped walking cane. The walnut skin of her be-ringed hands was wrinkled and blotched; her aquiline features were strongly masculine; she wore her black hair caught back into a tight chignon; when she greeted Una, apologised for her yesterday's absence, and asked for Una's impressions of her new home, her voice sounded as if it had grown used to tiredness and the indifference of despair.

Wondering whether, like Zante, she thought she knew her son had taken his own life, Una's heart ached for the additional pain which Una herself was convinced she need not suffer. That he had died by accident, rather than at his own hand, must surely be easier to bear, and Una resolved that, if the subject of Jason were not completely taboo, she would do her best to persuade his mother that the coroner's verdict had been the right one.

If she succeeded and Maria Diomed had any influence with Zante, that might help to sway his obsession with her own guilt. Though Una had little hope of it, the thought enabled her to answer Maria's questions with the eager enthusiasm to be expected of a new, happy bride. She scorned to look at Zante for his approval of her 'act', but his easy contributions and the light endearments he addressed to her, false though they sounded to her, were a kind of backcloth to her efforts. How he must be enjoying himself! she thought bitterly.

Her first intimation that, far from being taboo, the subject of her son's death was very much at the forefront of Maria's mind, came very shortly upon Una's congratulating the older woman on her command of spoken English. Maria answered dully, 'Thank you. As a girl, I spent six or seven years in England at school, and I visited it several times again during both my marriages. As a country, I loved it then. But now I shall never set foot in it again—never.'

'Oh surely, madame, if you loved it——!'

'Darling, really! ' Zante interposed lightly. 'I have made you her niece, so no more "madames" if you please! She doesn't allow me even the handle of "Aunt", so I'm sure she won't expect it of you either. Isn't it so, Maria?'

Maria nodded weary agreement. Una told her, 'Thank you,' and Maria, bypassing the interruption, repeated, 'Never,' and again, 'Never—after the way the English murdered my son! '

Several moments of utter stillness followed that. Una felt that Zante had tensed, but he said nothing and she did not know how to reply. Until at last she echoed, 'Murdered? Oh no, you mustn't allow yourself to think that—please! '

Maria's dark gaze fixed upon her. 'You knew Jason, Zante says?' she questioned.

'Yes. First, while he was at the University, and then——'

'So you know that some evil person accused him of a theft of which he wasn't guilty?'

'I—knew that a case was to be brought against him, yes.'

'And that, despairing of proving his innocence, he chose to take his life?'

'No! His death was due to an accident to his

car. The inquest brought it in so,' Una urged.

'He died for honour's sake,' Maria insisted. 'And for honour's sake, I wish no peace in this world for his accuser. Zante too—he will not rest either until Jason is avenged.'

Una shivered visibly. There was something almost diabolic about the belief these two held, that they had the right to revenge for an imaginary wrong. She remembered some writer's having described revenge as a kind of wild justice, and that was how they must see it—as justice to be done, when to the whole sane world they didn't share, it was the sin of revenge. She had little hope of diverting Zante from it, but at least she must try with Maria. If she could persuade his mother that no wrong had been done to Jason Mithredes, that might mean she had one enemy the less on this treacherously beautiful island.

She heard Zante dismissing the subject. 'You shouldn't expect Una to know very much of the circumstances, Maria. She was in Egypt when the case against Jason was due to come on, and she didn't return to England until after his death.'

'Is that so?' Maria grasped her cane, preparatory to leaving the table. 'Then you wouldn't know who was his enemy?' she asked Una.

The blunt question took Una unawares. In confusion she began, 'I—— That is——' then stopped. Let Zante get out of that one if he could! she thought in defiance.

He did. He said smoothly, 'Why should she? The police don't broadcast how and where they get their evidence.' To which Maria returned a listless, 'I suppose not,' before asking what were his plans for the day.

He told her he and Una would be meeting the Professor off the morning steamer. They would probably lunch in the town, and if Daniel were not too tired after his journey, he might like to investigate the archaeological site, and they would bring him back to the house to dine. Meanwhile the steamer would not be docking for an hour, and excusing himself to Una, he left the table with Maria.

At something of a loss to fill in the time, Una wandered out into the gardens where shrub beds terraced down to a foot-thick loose stone parapet, below which the terrain dropped more steeply to the road, and beyond that again down to the straggle of flat-roofed houses which were the outskirts of the town. From the parapet the closer view was of glossy greenery and shale pathways, and the far one was of the expanse of sea to the south of the island. Kassikona was a mere mound of rock, nestling in the clawlike embrace of the mother-island's most southerly headland. Una was remembering Homer's 'wine-dark sea' and thinking that in some lights it was indeed more purple and red-stained than blue, when footsteps skittered the pebbles of the path behind her and Zante was there at her side.

She did not look round nor up at him. He left her to her absorption in the view for a minute or two, then said, 'Debating ways of escape? Though need you? You are doing very well so far.'

She turned on him then. 'I've no means of escape,

as you know very well. And I'm doing my best, because I've no choice. But for pity's sake, if you have any, don't patronise me, *please*!' she exploded.

She might not have spoken. Zante went on, 'Your handling of Maria at breakfast was masterly. If you do as well by my father-in-law, you'll pass. Though, if I may say so, I take some credit myself in my role of having made you the sparkling, fulfilled bride of one white night of love. An adequate performance on my part, wouldn't you say?'

Una flamed to the sarcasm. 'Of course it was,' she pretended to agree. 'And why? Because you are *used* to deceit. You've made a study of it. You thrive on it, and it doesn't matter who is at the receiving end—me, or your aunt, or my father!'

'In their case, for their protection from learning the worst about you, my dear—that you accused and harried that boy to his suicide for reasons which perhaps you would prefer they shouldn't suspect.'

'Are you suggesting I went out of my way to accuse him? I only answered the questions the police asked. All the team was sleeping in hutments on the site; it was moonlight that night; I couldn't sleep, and when I went outside to get some air I saw Jason crossing to his own quarters, carrying the vase. Almost at once the night watchman gave the alarm, and when the police came I'd have perjured myself if I hadn't told them what I had seen. Anyway, what possible reason could I have had—or be ashamed of—for wanting to harm him?' she demanded.

Zante leaned, elbow to elbow with her, on the

parapet. Not looking at her, but at the view, 'I can think of an extremely powerful one,' he murmured. 'Are you quite sure your motives weren't those of "a woman scorned", as the poet has it?'

Una's fingers gripped the stone of the parapet until her knuckles showed white. 'There was never anything of—of that sort between Jason Mithredes and me,' she denied hotly.

'Just an idea,' Zante shrugged. 'From the enquiries I made, you and he were the only young people working on that project, and it would have been odd if you weren't at least sexually aware of each other, if not actually involved.'

'Odd or not, I wasn't involved.'

'Nor wanted to be—rather hopelessly, when you learned he already had a girl in England?'

'I didn't learn it. I wasn't interested enough to want to. And if he had one, how did *you* know about her?'

'More enquiries I made—for which I don't apologise. And so you stick by your story that you were only doing your duty as a citizen when you informed on Jason to the police?'

'I've told you before, I didn't inform on him. I only answered the police questions truthfully.'

'And only the gods know just how righteous the righteous can be!' Zante looked at his watch and straightened. 'Time we went down to the harbour. Come,' he said.

Although the steamer would not dock for a quarter of an hour, when they went out on to the quay, her bulk could already be seen in silhouette across the water. Zante introduced Una and chatted in Greek to the boatmen and dock-hands, for whom the arrival of the steamer was apparently the one event of the morning, since they filled in the waiting time with nothing more demanding than gossip over a little leisurely net-mending and drinking of ouzo at the dockside cafés.

When Daniel Keith came ashore he seemed stiff with fatigue and so grey of face that Una realised with a stab of pity how impossible it would have been to greet him with the stark news which Zante had forbidden he should hear. As she ran to hug him, she forced a radiantly welcoming smile. She was the new, happy bride of two days whom he would have been expecting to see; no cloud in her sky, no menace in the shape of Zante for either of them.

Although the sea-trip had tried him, he had had a good flight to Corfu, he said, and over a drink and luncheon, his energy and colour returned and he was eager to be taken out to the site, which, though it was several kilometres of zigzag climb from the town, was within level, reasonable walking distance of the White House. He inspected the area eagerly, questioned Zante as to the finds which had already been made, and stooped often to run samples of soil and pebbles through experimental, expert fingers.

'There's going to be plenty of preliminary work for me here,' he said. 'I'm going to miss badly my chief aide, my second-in-command, my deputy, my photographer, my labour-pool manager—— How many other maid-of-all-work roles do you fill for me, darling?' he wanted to know of Una.

She smiled, seeing a way of frequent escape from Zante, which she ought not to need, but did. 'Oh, I expect I shall find plenty of time to help you as I've always done,' she told him.

'*You* expect?' he took her up. 'My girl, surely that's for Zante to say! A new bride and groom— I'd be very surprised if for a long while to come, he won't let you out of his sight!'

Zante said with light banter, 'By that are you implying, sir, that at some time in the future, when I've done with her, you may take her back and welcome?'

Daniel laughed. 'I'm sorry, son. Did I make it sound like that?'

'Hideously,' said Zante. 'However, even in these first halcyon days, if she asks humbly enough, I might be persuaded to lend her to you from time to time. What are your immediate plans and needs?'

'Well——' Daniel looked about him, 'there's a lot to be done before we can begin to dig. I'll need labour for fencing off the area as the first move. Scale plans come next, and huts for storing specimens when there are any; dry storage for the equipment, the entrenching tools and trowels and tarpaulins, and a hut to act as an office where wages are paid and the drawing and written work done.'

'Looks as if you've weeks of work ahead of you before you unearth your first fragment,' Zante commented.

Daniel nodded. 'That's why it's important to get

on during the spring and summer before the winter
rains have a chance to spoil the site.'

'And where does Una come in on this scene?'
Zante asked.

'Mainly as photographer. She photographs site
boundaries and soil sections and later on, the finds.
In between she writes up the diary, acts as pay-clerk
and general keeper of the peace——'

'And I? What do I do?'

'You?' Daniel looked surprised.

'Why, don't you employ any enthusiastic ama-
teurs? Zante asked.

Daniel beamed. 'But of course you'd be welcome
—no one more so. I hadn't realised you'd have the
time or the interest——'

'In history being made on my own island? What
do you think?'

'We can't *know* we'll make any history, or even
find so much as a pottery shard,' Daniel warned.

'All the same, I've a right to a finger in the dish
you may never find,' Zante maintained. 'So, for a
start, what about my recruiting some local labour
for you?'

'If you would, I'd be very grateful.'

Their accord, Zante's and her father's, was so
complete that for the second time that day Una
knew that, though she had the right to shatter it,
she could not. While Daniel's happiness lay in the
recurring adventure of his work, she must not snatch
it from him. Sooner or later he would have to learn
that Jason Mithredes had been Zante's cousin, and
that both Zante and Jason's mother believed he had

comitted suicide. The Professor would deny the
possibility, as she had done. But the responsibility
for the prosecution case had been the Museum's,
not his, and though he would show sympathy for
Jason's mother, his deeper concern could justifi-
ably stop there, Una felt.

As long as he knew nothing of the sadistic penalty
Zante had exacted from her there would be no
threat to his peace of mind. He loved her; he had
loved her mother; he must know the kind of radi-
ance which love in all its aspects lent to a marriage
and while she could pretend she was experiencing
them all with Zante, he need not suffer, nor lose the
friend he believed Zante to be.

But how long could she maintain the cruel charade? How long must she monitor every word and
look? How long before the mask slipped and the
truth showed through?

CHAPTER THREE

WHEN they left the site Zante had suggested a tour of the island's tortuous roads, and after arranging the hire of a car for the Professor, they had taken him back to the house for dinner. On the drive Zante had prepared him for meeting Maria by saying she was a semi-invalid and a martyr to migraine. But that was all, and when at dinner no one referred to Maria's loss of her son, Una concluded that Zante had either said nothing more to Daniel later, or had warned him against provoking Maria to such a fury of bitterness as had upset her at breakfast. Una herself had had no time alone with her father in which to ask him what, if anything, Zante had said about Jason, recalling him and the circumstances of his death to Daniel's mind.

They moved to the salon for coffee and liqueurs. Maria went early to her room, and when Daniel was ready to leave, Zante told Una, 'We'll probably take a nightcap at the inn, so don't wait up for me, sweetheart, if you're tired,' and brushed her cheek with his lips.

Daniel kissed her more robustly. 'I'll not keep the man long, I promise,' he said. At which Zante quipped,

'On the second night of the man's honeymoon? Just try!'

And Daniel had once corrected himself when he had described Zante as two-faced! thought Una bitterly as they left her. If only Daniel knew ...

In her room she dawdled over unnecessary tasks, arguing that the later she went to bed, the shorter the lonely night. Even then she would read—she must, in an effort to crowd out thought. But in the excited flurry of departure, she had brought nothing with her, hardly expecting that she would need to read her nights away. There were books downstairs, but she hadn't inspected them for anything in English.

She had seen English popular paperbacks on the news-stands at Corfu airport. So perhaps Zante had some in his room. When he had first shown it to her, she hadn't noticed much but its bachelor character. But yes—when she opened the connecting door to it, she saw what she wanted—a shelf of paperbacks in Greek and French and English. She chose a best-selling thriller she had not read, and lingered, looking about her. At the bed where Zante had slept before he knew her; at the furniture he touched and used every day; at the room where she should have been free to run happily in and out, as he should have been equally welcome in hers ... theirs, to talk, to make love, to sleep and to wake, separate only by their shared will, not by the cruel barrier he had deliberately erected between them.

She stood flicking through the pages of the book, reading a few snatches here and there. Then, impatient of its problems which would all be neatly solved at the end, she knew she couldn't read, couldn't concentrate, and she thrust it back into its place on the shelf.

As she turned for the door her eye caught something on the broad window-shelf. Not a photograph, not a picture, but a pencil sketch fastened to a piece of hardboard only by paper-clips and supported by a hinged 'leg' of hardboard gummed to its back.

Below the drawing was scrawled 'Selene' and the signature was the entwined monogram Z.D. with which Zante signed his landscapes.

The few economical lines of the drawing showed a girl kneeling, sitting back on her heels, supporting herself on her spread hands. Her legs and feet were bare; her dress was a thigh-length shift, tied on the shoulders; her hair hung back from her upturned head; the profile of chin, nose and brow only barely suggested by the pencil.

Who was she? Una wondered jealously. And why hadn't her portrait been considered worthy of a frame? Strange, how a few skilled lines could *suggest* beauty without elaborating it on paper. For 'Selene', whoever she was, was beautiful in a classic way—all that Una herself was not.

She was in bed when she heard Zante come upstairs. She didn't suppose he meant to come in, but he did so just as she reached to switch off the bedside light, pretending she was asleep.

Her sorely tried nerves found an outlet in irritation. 'Do you think you have the right to walk into my room when you please?' she asked.

He strolled over to stand by the bed. 'You consider I'm taking liberties?'

'In the circumstances.'

'Of my having given you my name, and the freedom of my house and a respect you don't deserve, but will accrue to you as my wife? Not to mention a financial settlement on you which I've already put in hand? In those circumstances, aren't I entitled to some care for your physical wellbeing?'

'If you really cared about that, you wouldn't deny me the one thing that makes nonsense of your having provided all the rest.'

'You mean the one thing known as "love"?'

She nodded over her absorption in pleating the edge of the sheet with nervous fingers. 'It ought to be implicit in marriage, and I thought it was in ours. You let me believe it. You pretended you wanted me as . . . as I wanted you. If you hadn't——' Her voice broke wretchedly.

His regard of her was thoughtful. 'Yes,' he agreed. 'A pity that I realised from the start that you weren't the gold-digger type who would fall for a dangled bank-balance as bait. You needed some romantic element to my courtship of you. So I supplied it, and must, as we agreed for our own good reasons, go on supplying it for public consumption. In other words, a husband who isn't seen or known to frequent his wife's room with eager regularity—well, that makes the whole marriage suspect to gossip. And that we can't have, can we?'

'You mean *you* can't have it.'

'You too. If you didn't see the wisdom of going along with the situation, you'd have put the Professor back on that steamer this morning, and have gone with him.'

'There was no "wisdom" involved,' she retorted bitterly. 'You gave me no choice.'

He nodded slowly. 'Good—as long as you recognise that you have no choice. But are you sure it's only I who am denying it to you?'

She didn't understand. 'Of course it's you. Who else?'

'Yourself, I'd have thought. After all, in our affair, if you hadn't wanted to believe quite badly that my courting of you was genuine, shouldn't I have been wasting my time? In other words, you were a willing enough victim, and to a certain degree, are still. Am I right?'

Una longed to hate him for knowing so much about her. Instead she could only hate herself for letting her love be so transparent, so committed. She questioned gropingly, 'You are saying that I'm not only concerned for Father, but that—that you don't fear I may leave you, because you suspect I love you still?' And then, with a pitiful attempt at bravado, 'Really! Just how vain can you get?'

He ignored the flippancy. 'Not necessarily that you love me,' he said. '*That* you've probably already switched off. But having believed you had me at your feet, like any woman, you aren't going to pass up any chance of getting me there again. Therefore you will stay without too much duress from me, while you have some hope of that.' He paused, stepped nearer, lifted the dark fall of her hair and spread it fanwise on her pillow. As she shivered in recoil and flung it over to her far shoulder out of his reach, he mused, 'All that young allure going to waste! If I weren't immune, I might almost be tempted——'

She broke in. 'Go away. Please go away!' she begged huskily.

He went. But at the door she checked him. 'Who is Selene?' she asked.

Zante stopped and turned. 'A girl,' he said.

'Yes, but who? There's a drawing of her in your room——'

His brows lifted. 'I've no right to intrude in your room, but you can make free of mine?'

She flushed. 'That's different. You weren't there. I was afraid of not sleeping, so I went to see if you had any English books I could read. I didn't take one, but there was this sketch you had made of "Selene", and I wondered who she was.'

' "Is",' he corrected. 'She is of the present, not the past. Her name is Selene Trepano, she is nineteen years old; her family dates from the Venetian occupation of Corfu; she has modelled for me. Is that enough of a thumbnail sketch?'

'You said you didn't use models!' Una accused.

'Nor do I, in the ordinary sense. Nor paint portraits, as you know. But occasionally I need a human figure to point up a landscape, and I've made a series of Selene in different poses so that I can use them as and when I need. The one in my room is typical.'

'She's very beautiful,' Una said with difficulty.

'She has style and line, and can take up any pose one suggests to her.'

'Does she live on the island?'

'No, in Corfu Town, in a crumbling palace with her widowed mother, a true *grande dame,* with illusions of a wealth her husband squandered years ago. Selene pilots an ugly-tempered speedboat when she comes over here. You'll meet her some time or other.'

Una thought back. 'Was she the girl in silhouette on the rocks in your painting, *Thalassa, thalassa!*?' she asked.

'Yes. She is a natural for any sea subject—as lithe as a mermaid and as elusive as spilled quicksilver. And she is glad of the money for working for me.'

'And is she one of the women you warned me you could turn to when you are tired of being celibate?' The tart question had gone beyond recall, almost before Una had formed it.

Zante opened the door and moved to the threshold. 'Don't be shrewish. It doesn't become you,' he advised icily, 'Meanwhile, you may be very sure that if or when I take Selene Trepano or any other woman to my bed, I shall do it with the utmost discretion. Your public status as my wife won't be affected at all.' The door closed softly, and he was gone. *Knowing he can always defeat me with scorn, if with nothing worse,* she thought bitterly as she faced another lonely night.

Zante did not come to her room the next morning, and when she went downstairs he was already at the breakfast table. His aunt did not appear. Una, diffident and nervous, marvelled at the self-assured urbanity of his manner after the acid rebuke with which he had parted from her overnight.

They were served by a young maid with whom he joked. A gardener, brushing the burnt grass of a lawn, was within earshot, and Zante was playing to them both, as he was to her with the consummate ease of a happily married groom at breakfast with his bride. Oddly, his poise was infectious, and presently she was asking his advice about her day, as if nothing more important were troubling either of them.

'Would you like me to begin to get to know your staff, and to find out how much responsibility Madame Di—— I mean Maria—would like me to take over, if any?' she asked him.

He shook his head. 'There's no need. Let it all happen. The house can run itself while you have so little of the language. But modern Greek isn't too difficult, and you'll get by with a few basic words and phrases for the time being. No, I expected you would want to go over to the site.'

'I'd like to, though there isn't much point until the stores and the gear Father had sent by freight come in. Might they today, do you think? Does the steamer call?'

'Always, when there's something to be offloaded. We'll collect your father, and go to the Port Office to see if it has received any advice about the stuff.' Zante crumpled his napkin and stood up. 'Whenever you are ready?' he invited.

At the Port Office there was news that the gear had been shipped and would be arriving on the steamer. So the three of them joined the groups of gossipmongers on the quay to await the steamer's docking. Daniel planned to take the precious cases to his lodging for checking and safe keeping until the less valuable tools and equipment could be kept under cover at the site.

The steamer was still on the horizon when the busy beat of a motor craft became the predominant sound above the quayside noises of clanking chains and the slap of oars and the grinding of moored boats at their berths. Then a speed-launch came curvetting across the bay to hurl itself at the jetty wall almost without perceptible check to its pace as it came alongside and its engine was cut.

A girl in white slacks and navy-blue shirt stood up in it and beckoned to a dockhand to take the mooring rope which she threw up to him. Zante had stood too and was there to meet her as she mounted the jetty steps. She thrust her sunglasses up to ride on her long russet hair and tucked her arm intimately into his as he brought her to introduce her to Daniel and Una.

Una's instinct had already said *Selene Trepano* before Zante spoke, for this girl's lithe figure was that of the sketch in his room, and of the nymph on the rocks in his seascape which he had titled, *The Sea, the Sea!* Was this a chance visit to Erikona? Or at Zante's invitation? And when he had said Selene was of his present, not his past, what had he meant her to read into that? Una wondered as she took the slim hand which was offered to her, without interruption to the eager chatter in Greek with which the girl was plying Zante.

Zante reproved her. 'Speak English. My wife doesn't understand Greek,' he told her.

Evidently his introduction of Una was slow to penetrate, for Selene stared open-mouthed, dropped her hand as if it were a scorpion, and questioned Zante again in Greek.

He answered in the same language, then urged, 'Come along, show what you can do. Now start again.' He turned to Una. 'Una darling, this is Selene of whom I've told you. And Selene, meet Una, my wife, and don't pretend you hadn't heard from Maria that I was bringing her home with me.'

Selene made an effort. 'Madame Diomed has not told me,' she said in careful, slow English. 'I do not come over while you are in England, so I do not see her. Therefore, how do I hear you have married? You send a postcard—two—of horse-soldiers in tall fur hats, but you do not tell this, nor when you return.'

'Then what brought you over here this morning? Witch's sight?' he countered.

Selene shrugged. 'I hear it in a café somewhere—that Kyrios Diomed of Erikona is back, bringing guests, a lady and——' Her glance went to Daniel and Zante repeated the introduction of him which he had already made.

She bobbed gracefully—'Kyrios Keith,' she acknowledged Daniel, and returned her scrutiny to Una, who smiled and complimented her, 'You speak English very well. Better than I speak any foreign language. How did you learn it?'

Selene shrugged again. 'We have many English tourists in Corfu, and when my mother has no money, we have guests who pay us, and I learn from them when I cook and serve them at their table. I learn from Zante too—*much* from Zante, do I not?' she appealed to him.

'As much as it is good for you to know,' he humoured her. 'And now you are here, what are we going to do with you?'

The girl's mobile lips thrust forward in a little pout. 'I think that now you have come back you will—want me,' she said. 'Do you not?'

In view of Zante's employment of her as a model, the question, at surface level, was innocent enough. But Una's distrust and jealousy read a sinister double meaning into its hesitant phrasing. In what way had Selene expected Zante to 'want' her? And if she hadn't meant to insult his wife by asking, why hadn't she done so in a language she knew Una would not understand? The suspicion continued to rankle, even though Zante's reply was a robust, 'Not today, little one. I've work to do for our friend here'—indicating Daniel—'and I shall not be "wanting" you.' (Putting the word that mattered into quote-marks for my benefit! thought Una. Knowing I'm remembering last night, and enjoying tantalising me!)

Selene asked, 'Work? What work?'

Zante explained that when the steamer, now in dock, had unloaded, he would be touring the island, recruiting the labour he had promised Daniel he would find.

'And may I come with you?' Selene urged.

Zante looked with raised eyebrows at Una, who said quickly, 'I must help Father to check the gear,' saving Zante the trouble of suggesting they make a threesome, saving herself any further humiliation at Selene Trepano's hands.

She and Daniel had counted and sorted the various items of their stock-in-trade—the trowels, the prismatic compasses, the ranging poles and pegs, the entrenching tools, the theodolite, Una's precious camera, which she claimed lovingly—the reference books, the measuring tapes, the piles of graph paper —and were enjoying a well-earned drink on the terrace of his taverna.

Daniel asked, 'And how are the first days of her marriage going for my girl?'

Glad that he hadn't asked how she was enjoying them, Una said, 'Everything is so strange, so different, that I hardly know how to answer that. I mean— only three days ago I wasn't married, I was in England with you, and it was trying to snow—in April! —and now we're both here in this place which is so fantastic that I find myself wondering whether it's real and whether any of it has happened. Cloud Nine—that's where I'm at for the moment, and finding it a pretty dizzy height to be, believe me!'

As an evasion, it had been a poor effort, she knew, and evidently Daniel found it so. He picked up his glass and peered through the amber liquid it contained.

He said, 'It was *marriage*, love, that I was asking about. Whether the reality comes up to the dream— or is it too early to expect you to know?'

'About—Zante?'

'About being married to him, instead of just engaged. It's a change that could be a shock for a girl, and I should hate it to have been one for you.'

If only she could tell him how great a shock this marriage had been! She agreed, 'Yes, I see that it could be. But not, surely, when the girl is quite sure that she loves the man and always will?'

'Even though she could have expected too much and felt disappointed?' Daniel mused.

Una managed a laugh. 'What are you trying to make me say, you wretch of a parent, you?' she teased. 'That I'm feeling a bit let down by my experience of married bliss?'

'M'm—a degree of anti-climax would be understandable, I'd have thought,' Daniel murmured.

'As if, after only three days, I'd be entitled to a grievance, even if I had one!' she mocked, and watched the concern clear from his face.

He laid a hand over hers. 'Just wondering, girl, that's all,' he said. 'Don't take any notice of me.'

He wondered aloud next as to how successful Zante might be over drumming up labour for the site, then asked, 'That young naiad who arrived in the speedboat—what do we know about her?'

Una told him.

'His model? I didn't know he used any. Did you?' Daniel questioned.

'He doesn't, in the ordinary way. Only when he feels a figure will do something for a landscape, he says.'

'She seemed rather taken aback by you; that you and he were married, I thought.'

'Well, as he only seems to have sent her a couple of picture-postcards from England, she probably would be surprised, wouldn't she?' Una said, as casually as she could.

'Or shocked—depending on how intimate she had thought they were before you appeared——' Daniel broke off to point to the road and to finish his drink at a gulp. 'There! That's Zante's car. Now, let's hope, we're in business.'

Zante had been alone. Selene had gone back to Corfu, he said. He had reported having collected a team of labourers for the preliminary fencing and digging, a couple of carpenters for the building of the huts and had enlisted the interest of one or two leisured, responsible friends who would make the nucleus of a team of excavators when the time came for the careful, skilled work which Daniel planned.

They had lunched before repairing to the site, where Zante and Una had shared Daniel's eager pottering and measuring and marking out during the long scorching afternoon, and the sun was a golden ball in the west before they dropped Daniel at his lodgings. As they parted from him, Zante asked Una in his hearing whether she would care for a swim.

He couldn't want to swim with her, hating her as he did. His 'Darling, what about a dip before we go home?' in front of Daniel could only have been to impress Daniel with his need to be with her all the time. If she refused, he would let Daniel hear him teasing her lovingly into agreeing, so upon a perverse impulse to cheat him of that sham pleasure, she accepted, only offering the excuse that she hadn't her swimsuit with her.

'No problem. I've been back to the house and fetched it for you,' he said. Daniel beamed and waved them away, and Una said tautly,

'I suppose I've got to accept that that's part of the charade you're making me play—parading the things people would expect us to want to do together as if you really *wanted* to do them with me, which you can't.'

He glanced at her along his shoulder, his eyes lazily hooded. 'Congratulations,' he drawled. 'You are learning fast. I haven't had to fault you yet. And who are you to say I can't want to swim with you? For the record, I don't care for swimming alone. No challenge. No competition to it. None of the stimulation, the spice, to swimming with an attractive girl.'

'With *any* attractive girl.' She made a flat statement of it, not a question.

'Though with an attractive wife available to me, why should I trouble to look further?' he countered. '*I* wanted to swim; I suspect you did too. So what was wrong in getting your father's blessing on the innocent enterprise?'

'There was nothing innocent about it. You deliberately planned to deceive him!'

'Guilty, yes. But a necessary touch in the circumstances. And I'm afraid you are going to have to suffer seeing and hearing more of the same if we are to keep him happy. And that we agreed he had to be, didn't we?'

Through set lips she retorted, 'He *was* happy and would have stayed that way, if you'd left us both alone and behind you in England!'

'Ah, but that you should stay happy in your bogus good conscience wasn't in my plan at all, you see. I thought I'd already made that abundantly clear?'

At that she suddenly saw red. 'You have,' she assured him. 'In the crudest, most despicable way. And now, as I refuse to drive any further with you today, please stop to let me get out, and I'll walk home.'

His hands remained immovably on the wheel, his foot on the accelerator. 'You'll do nothing of the kind,' he said. 'We are going swimming. *You* are going swimming, even if I have to strip you to the buff and pour you into the bit of nonsense which passes for a provocative form of *cache-sexe*——' He ignored her sharp-drawn gasp of distaste. '—*And* you will join with me afterwards in assuring any interested party that we both enjoyed ourselves enormously. Do you understand?'

She disdained to answer, and sat, ostensibly watching the road and the scenery, but aware in every fibre of his tantalising physical nearness—the proud Grecian profile turned to her, the body she could have touched and caressed, simply by stretching a hand, the easy assured movements dictated by his brain—and all of it as distant and removed from her as the galaxy by his inner, essential withdrawal from her. Marriage! One of the loveliest of words—and more empty and meaningless for them than the most inept of dumbshow.

Zante parked on the small lay-by of a road above a crescent of sandy beach, studded by boulders just licked at their bases by wavelets. Una had to accept his help over the rocky path leading down to the shore, but walked alone to the shadow of the biggest boulder in order to change. He stood just short of the tidemark on the sand, kicked off his sandals, stripped himself of shirt and slacks, showing he wore swimming-briefs underneath, then ran into the surf, waded and plunged.

He swam out strongly until all she could see of him was his golden head and the raised arm of his crawl-stroke. By the time he came back she was in the water herself, revelling in its silky warmth and, almost against her will, feeling her rancour lessen and temporarily drop away.

It was impossible not to smile when he porpoise-dived and came up beside her, the golden hair plastered and the sapphire eyes flicking water from their lashes. Nor openly to shrug away when, with one hand on her shoulder, he urged her to swim beside him until, as at the same impulse, they turned to float, staring up into a sky which at that hour had lost its noonday whiteness of heat and was streaked with the gold and purple rays of the dying sun. Una had resented his categorical ruling that it was pleasant to swim in company; had been jealous of the women who had played and competed with him, but he was right. This swim, welcome as it was, wouldn't have been the same without Zante's beloved body curvetting and circling and plunging and inviting her—even though the invitation was empty of any welcome that mattered to her heart.

When they left the water he walked over to her boulder with her and, taking her towel from her, dried her hair. Surprised that he should want to touch her in any personal way, she stood still under the attention, but found the nonchalance with which he threw the towel back to her when he had finished much more in character with his contempt of her when there was no one there as witness. She had tingled with desire at the touch of his hands on the sensitive flesh of her neck. But he would have given pains to the drying-down of a wet dog in much the same way. And he wouldn't have despised the dog ...

Selene Trepano was not mentioned until they were at dinner that evening with Maria, who picked at her food, stared with lacklustre eyes into the middle distance between mouthfuls, and spoke very little. Until, when Zante said casually, 'Selene Trepano came over in *Thetis* this morning,' she seemed to spark into life, as at an electric shock.

'Selene Trepano! *That* trash!' She almost spat the words.

Zante's anger turned upon her as Una had known it to turn upon herself. 'Selene is *not* trash. Kindly guard your tongue, Maria,' he ordered her.

She ignored him. She put down her fork and pushed aside her plate. 'Trash! Trash! *Trash!*' she repeated in an almost hysterical shriek, reminding

Una of a child in a vicious temper, goading a parent as far as it dared. Una glanced at Zante. His lips were compressed in a hard line, his eyes stormy. Maria appealed to her,

'You have met this little—tramp? This one'—the jerk of her head indicated Zante—'he has told you what she did to Jason? My Jason, who worshipped her and whom she scorned and drove away? If it hadn't been for *her*, he would never have left me here alone. Never have gone to your accursed country to be murdered by one of you—the one whom Zante—since I cannot—should hound down and force to suffer as Jason must have suffered in his spirit before he took honour's way out—and died.' She paused to draw a tortured breath. 'But no,' she continued, 'he would not have told you this, for now she has *him* in her thrall too! You did not know this, did you, little English girl, with your innocent face and the quiet manner of a nun?' Suddenly her features contorted and now her fury was for Una as she demanded, 'Though why should I pity you? You are English, are you not? English, and therefore base. *And you knew Jason.*' Her eyes narrowed to mere slits of darkness. 'So how do *I* know that it wasn't you—or you with others—who drove him to his death?' She burst into wild, abandoned tears.

As Una drew a sharp breath of horror, Zante acted. He ordered her, 'Go to your room. I'll come to you there,' and went round the table to take Maria by her shoulders, to draw her to her feet and to guide her, stumbling and protesting, out of the room.

Una followed them up the stairs to where the landing divided for Maria's suite. She went on alone and sank down upon her bed, bent over her hands clasped between her knees, shivering in an ague of misery.

Now Zante would have to let her go! It made no difference that Maria did not know the truth of their marriage. From her own bitterness she had dredged up enough hatred of all that Una herself stood for, to make it impossible for her to stay. Daniel would have to know ... At the thought her heart seemed to turn over in pity for him. He had hoped so much for his work; been so happy for her. And now——!

The door opened and Zante came in, paused with his back to the door, saying nothing. She stood and ran to him in panic, beat with both fists at his chest. 'That—that was horrible, horrible!' she clamoured.

He took her hands by the wrists and pulled them down. 'I warned you. You see what she can be like,' he said.

'But I'd said nothing, done nothing to provoke her!'

'Only, this time, by your being there, being English, and therefore an irritant to her obsession about Jason.'

'And who brought me, to be lashed and accused through no fault of mine? You did,' Una accused. 'And as for her obsession, she is no more obsessed than you were when you married me for revenge.'

He corrected coldly, 'My obsession, as you call it, had purpose and reasons behind it. A purpose which I've carried out.'

'And look where it has led you—*and* me!'

'Led me?' he echoed. 'No further, so far, my dear, than I meant to go. Nothing about the situation has changed.'

She took a step backward and stared up at him. 'You can't be serious? You must know you've failed. Now that your aunt suspects me, how can you expect us ever to meet normally again? No, Zante Diomed'—she could not keep a bubble of triumph from her voice—'you know it's finished and that you'll have to let me go!'

There was a tense moment of silence which frightened her. Then his iron grip upon her wrist thrust her back on to the bed, where he moved to stand over her. 'I know nothing of the kind,' he said. 'With none of my purpose and no facts to go upon, Maria was only threshing out wildly at any victim within range of her despair—unfortunately, you.'

'She knows I knew Jason, and she suspects me. You'll have to tell her the truth.'

'And expose you to her justified wrath when she hears it? You have seen what she is like without cause, so do you suppose I'd turn you over to her when she has enough cause for savagery to vent it all on you?'

'But I shouldn't be here. If you have any mercy in you at all, you would have sent me back to England before that,' Una urged.

'*And* the Professor with you? Had you thought about him?'

In her frenzy to escape, she hadn't. 'He will have to know, but he will understand,' she claimed faintly. But she had crumpled, physically and mentally, and when Zante's head moved slowly from side to side, she knew that she had lost.

He mimicked her cruelly. 'Oh no, Una—Diomed,' he said. 'You are going nowhere away from here, and nor is your father. But somewhere you are going—and now, tonight—is to comfort Maria and convince her that you are indeed as innocent and nun-like as she has thought you so far, and will again if you try hard enough.'

'Zante, I can't! In her present mood, she'll refuse to see me. And what am I to say to her, even if she will? Or'—on a dying flare of defiance—'do you suggest I tell her that as far as you're concerned I *am* no more nor less than a——?'

She was stopped on the belittling word by Zante's fingers clamping smartly across her mouth. 'You'll not tell her that, not because I forbid it, but for the shame of it,' he stated as a fact of which he was sure.

The defiance flickered once more. 'Whose shame —mine or yours?' she demanded.

'Since there is nothing you can do about it, and I can, any time I please, surely yours?' he replied unanswerably. And then, 'Come, I'll take you to Maria's door.'

She went with him, defeated.

CHAPTER FOUR

THERE was no answer to Una's knock. She knocked again, waited and then ventured to open the door. Maria was sitting in a highbacked chair, one bony-knuckled hand on the head of her cane, the fingers of the other plucking idly at her skirt. When Una, on the threshold, asked 'May I come in?' Maria looked at her with none of her earlier hostility, in fact, almost without recognition.

Una found an embossed leather pouffe and sat on it, and when after a few minutes Maria was still looking at her in silence, she dared to put her hand over the restless fingers and still them.

She said, 'You were taken ill at dinner. Are you better now? Does your head ache? Zante is anxious about you, and he sent me to see if there was anything I could do for you.'

Maria withdrew her hand, but it ceased fidgeting. 'I was not ill at dinner. I was upset,' she said with dignity. 'Zante deliberately upset me, as he always knows he can with talk of that *petite amie* of his, the girl Trepano, whom he knows I have reason to hate.'

Una said, 'I don't think he wanted to upset you by mentioning that she came over from Corfu this morning, after hearing that he was back.'

'Then he must have meant to upset *you*.' Maria

peered down searching Una's face. 'For you are his English bride, are you not? The girl he married when he was last over there?'

Pitying but giving thanks for the confusion of mind which, it seemed, was to spare her the older woman's further abuse, Una told her, 'Yes. But I'm sure Zante didn't mean to annoy me either. For he had told me already that he used a girl named Selene Trepano as a model, and he introduced us when she arrived in her speedboat as he and my father and I were on the quay, waiting for the steamer.'

Maria's lip curled. 'Introduced her to his wife— that he should dare!'

'But why not?' Una urged. 'They are obviously friends, and it would have been even more odd if he hadn't introduced her to us, surely?'

'You may be very sure that they are more than friends,' Maria hinted darkly.

Neither sure nor unsure but hoping against, Una said, 'Oh, I don't think so. For one thing, she's very young.'

'And was younger still when she ensnared my son. There is no age limit for wantons like her. She teased him and provoked him and then cast him off when she began to covet Zante instead.' Maria sat back, her lips pursed. 'No, my dear, if you do not use all your feminine wiles to keep Zante now you have him, you could well lose him to those of a Circe like the Trepano girl, you may be certain of that—too late.'

Bewildered but relieved by this switch from wild vituperation to kindly patronage, Una said, 'I think you are mistaken, Madame, but if you thought it necessary, thank you for warning me, all the same.'

Maria bent forward again to touch her cheek. '"Madame"! "Madame"? What is this?' she chided. 'Did Zante not tell you I am "Maria", your kinswoman, as I am his?'

'Yes, I'm sorry,' Una murmured.

'That is good. And though Zante is wealthy and successful and has only to want a woman to get her, perhaps you are right and I am wrong, and you are confident that the same innocence which won him for you will keep him. If that is so, I am happy for you, child,' Maria finished with a wintry smile which wrung Una's heart.

She stood up. 'And you are all right now?' she questioned awkwardly. 'No longer as upset as you were with Zante?'

'As upset as I shall always be at mention or reminder of that—harpy. But with Zante, whom I can always forgive much, not any more—this time,' Maria said regally, and then with a languid gesture towards an embroidered bellpull at the door, 'Ring for my maid, please, child, as you go out. And I wish you a happy night,' she gave Una her dismissal.

Zante was waiting in her room as Una expected he would be. 'Well?' he asked impatiently.

She leaned back against the door she had closed behind her. 'It's all right. She's forgotten she'd turned on me,' she told him wearily.

He nodded slowly. 'I'd hoped so. It's typical,' he said.

'Typical?'

'Of her switches of mood and reasoning. As I told you, she has nothing against you personally, and that is how it must be—for both your sakes. She has to believe you are what you seem—my well-cherished bride, or there will be no peace for any of us.'

'You must have risked that when you brought me here——'

'Not if I schooled you properly first, as I have done, and so far, I'm glad to say, you have seen the prudence of responding.'

Una flared at the arrogance of that. ' "Schooled"!' she echoed. 'I'm not an animal you've put in training to be—be patted and encouraged when you consider it has done well, and whipped when it has not!'

Zante's brows went up. Hands in pockets, he strolled towards her. 'Strong words,' he commented. 'Have I ever threatened to whip you?'

Her cheeks flamed. 'You've implied that you—could.'

'H'm—coarse of me, under stress. No, I understand the best trainers advise only the lightest touch of the whip, if any, to get results. And after all, there are more pleasurable ways of bringing a *woman* to heel, are there not?'

She realised from his expression that he knew he had made his meaning understood. How he must hate her, to taunt her so! 'There'd be nothing pleasurable for either of us, if you dared to try,' she muttered. 'As I think I've told you already.'

'So you have,' he agreed. 'But don't worry. Hav-

ing merited a pat for placating Maria, you're in no
danger for the moment. Meanwhile, what had she
to say about or against Selene?'

'Whatever it was, you'd asked for it,' Una retorted
tartly.

'Yes, I mocked the gods by mentioning the child,
I know. But what did Maria say?'

'That Selene had thrown over Jason, which was
why he went to England, and for which she—Maria
—had reason to hate her. And that'—Una swal-
lowed hard—'you and Selene were more than the
—friends I took you to be. She warned me that I
could well lose you to Selene, not knowing, of
course, that I've never had anything of you that I
could value and—would fight to keep,' she concluded drearily.

So far he had only threatened her with an 'if or
when' time when he might betray her with Selene
or other women. But surely, if he had any pity, he
would tell her whether that time was imminent or
even now? But he did not. 'And you gave Maria to
believe you were equal to the risk?' he asked.

'I think so. I hope so. She hates Selene so much
that it seemed to reassure her.'

'You loyally defended me and the strength of our
marriage?'

'Which doesn't exist. But yes, I tried,' Una admitted.

As he came on and she had to stand aside for him
to reach the door, he reached to put a finger and
thumb to her chin, tilting it. 'Then *two* pats for

diplomacy. You've missed your vocation,' he said, and went out.

He did not come to her room nor was at breakfast the next morning. She took it alone without comment, ashamed to let the maid who served her guess that she did not know where he was. Afterwards she went to the garage to find his car was not there, and then to his room and through to his studio, where open cupboard doors and a scatter of small canvases and paint tubes on the bench suggested that he had gone painting. She remembered how she had teased him that she would insist on accompanying him. Well, times had changed since then, and now he hadn't given her the chance, nor even told her where he would be.

Realising that her father would almost certainly be at the site, she decided to walk over to join him. From a cotton shirt and shorts and sandals, she changed into a jumpsuit and stout boots and went to the kitchens where, by dint of pointing at foods and naming the few of which she knew the Greek names, she persuaded the willing and smiling cook to make up a picnic meal. *Fetta* she knew to be goats' cheese, and *taramosalata* was a fish-paste to spread on the bread she pointed out. Fruit was easy, for there were piles of oranges and large misshapen tomatoes, in bowls, and the cook offered an assortment of crisp biscuits and cakes. But when Una asked for lemonade as a drink, she recoiled in horror.

'*Gazzoza? Gazzoza? Okki, okki*—no, no!' she exclaimed, and made an effort in English. 'The Kyrios Zante—wine for him, *gazzoza*—no! He not take—never!' she explained, showing Una that it was assumed she was making a picnic for herself and Zante, instead of for herself and Daniel.

Una gave in and nodded Yes to the bottle of red wine which was added to the satchel of food before it was handed over with a smiling *Andio*, which was echoed by both the other maids in the kitchen.

She debated telling Maria where she was going, but decided against disturbing her. She left a note for Zante in her room; at least *she* wasn't discourteous to leave him to guess where she was!

It was a picturesque, scented walk across the hillslopes. The one or two cottages she passed were a dazzle of whitewashed walls; the one or two driven donkeys she met wore straw bonnets and decorated saddles, and the air smelled of the sea and the all-pervading scent of rosemary and thyme and myrtle. Prickly pear and cactus flourished on arid rock, and everywhere were the gnarled, twisted boles of the olive trees. Before she reached the site she could see the business afoot. Daniel was there, surrounded by a group of men. He was pointing and gesticulating; the men were nodding their understanding, and as she drew nearer she could hear that Zante had provided him with an interpreter among the gang of labourers he had enlisted.

Daniel protested at Una's arrival. 'Why aren't you with Zante?' he wanted to know. But he was obviously glad of her help, and very soon he had her photographing the limits of the site and discussing with him the best locations for the huts.

At noon the labourers all knocked off, as if summoned to their siesta by a factory siren. They vanished into the shade, the interpreter came to tell Daniel that they would work again at fourteen hours, and Daniel and Una shared their meal and drank the wine of which Daniel highly approved. Una did not tell him it had been chosen for Zante's palate, not his, and though she told him Zante had gone painting, she managed to avoid admitting she did not know where.

They both drowsed. Una came to, prepared to deny she had slept, at the stutter of a car bucketing on the stony perimeter of the site. Zante perhaps? But when the car stopped, it was a stranger who got out and picked his way across the site, looking about him. He was in shirt and shorts; young, darker of hair than Zante, lightly bearded, his shoulders slung about with camera case and binoculars. Una touched her father on the hand. 'Someone looking for you, I think,' she said.

Daniel sat up and rubbed his eyes. 'Who? What?' he was asking as the young man spotted them and came over to them.

He glanced from Daniel to Una and back again. 'Professor Keith?' he asked. 'You don't know me, but I'm Roland Luard, staying with my Greek friends, the Elmerios, and the link is Zante Diomed, who called on them yesterday while I was out, to say that you would be glad of help on your project when you get it going. And if so, I'd like to volunteer, if I may. I'm pretty fluent in Greek, if that counts for anything,' he added as an afterthought.

His voice was unmistakably English, and Daniel, though still slightly bemused by sleep, was eager to welcome him.

'Delighted to have you,' he said, and introduced Una to him. 'My daughter Una, my aide-de-camp, as it were, and just married to my son-in-law, Zante Diomed, as you probably know.'

The young man nodded. 'Yes, Mr and Mrs Elmerio had heard he was married in England and were disappointed that he hadn't brought Mrs Diomed with him when he called yesterday.' He took Una's proffered hand. 'Seems I'm ahead of them. Lucky me,' he smiled. 'And lucky Zante, come to that.'

Una took the easy compliment at its surface value, knowing that with her tousled hair and functional suit and boots, she could be no deserving object of gallantry. He was probably labelling her as a tedious blue-stocking and wondering what Zante had seen in her ...

Daniel was saying, 'As you see, we're only just planning the site, nowhere near the excavating stage yet. But I shall be grateful for any help you can give, particularly with my Greek, which is by no means always understood. You're on holiday, you say?'

'Not really,' Roland Luard told him. 'I'm on a six-months' sabbatical, doing my post-graduate thesis on the culture of twentieth-century Greece, studying on the mainland and the principal islands for so many weeks at a time. I'm staying here with Dana and Petro Elmerio, and I commute when necessary to Corfu by the steamer or by caique, but I can be free to help you at almost any time. I've done a bit of excavating with a holiday group in Sussex, but no classical work at all, and I'd like to.'

'Good,' said Daniel. 'Are you prepared to stay now?'

Roland threw a wry smile at Una. 'I thought he would never ask me!' he joked, and to Daniel, 'I'm all yours till sunset. Roll out the work.'

Daniel became immediately practical. Indicating the camera, 'You are a photographer?' he asked.

'Amateur only.'

'That's good enough. I have to do some more readings to establish the perimeter; the men will follow me up, doing their fencing work, and then you and Una can get the result on film. That will be enough for today. Meanwhile, while you are waiting—how good a Boy Scout were you?' Daniel broke off to ask.

A grin. The bearded youth had a winning smile, Una decided. 'Patrol leader. Badge glutton. Why do you ask?'

'Then you and Una can put up a tent for our temporary use until we get our first hut. You'll find all the doings over there, among the stores. Una will show you where——' And Daniel left then to go to meet his returning team.

Roland regarded his retreating back with respect. 'They say the true mark of leadership is the ability to delegate duty to other people. Does the Professor always expect you to muscle in on any old job that needs to be done?' he asked.

Una smiled. 'Since I've been helping him, I've had to tackle most of the "any old jobs" there are. Come along, we'd better get the hang of this tent.'

'You always work for him on his digs?'

'On several of them; some of them for his own research, some for the FalconbridgeMuseum. He has a chair at the University.'

'Yes, so I heard. Where have you worked?'

'In England, on Roman remains; once in Sicily, in Ireland, Egypt, and now here————'

'But I thought Dana Elmerio understood that, though Zante had brought you straight home to Erikona, you were still in your honeymoon days?'

Hidden in the question was an implied one which good manners hadn't asked, but which Una made haste to answer.

'So we are,' she said. 'But knowing how Father depends on me, my husband was terribly generous and offered to take himself on a painting trip today.' (Well, Zante had offered to lend her to Daniel from time to time, hadn't he? So perhaps the bluff of her claim was only half a lie.)

'H'm—more generous than I'd be on my honeymoon, considering————' commented her companion. (*But you are not Zante Diomed. And we are not on honeymoon. And I'm not Zante's wife.*) For one wild moment Una was tempted to shock this bland young man with the stark truth that only she and Zante knew. But instead she asked, 'Have you met my husband? Do you know him?'

'Only by repute. That his painting is acclaimed everywhere; that this island is his heritage from way back; that he is virtually king of it, you might say—and now, that he has married within his proper station. For "Una" is a princess kind of a name, I've always thought. Haven't you?' Roland appealed.

'Have you?' Una said non-committally.

'*And* an only-daughter name. Are you the Professor's only child?'

She told him she was, and they began to sort out the gear they needed for the tent. He chose a site for it and organised its erection with workmanlike precision. Una acted as his mate, handing supports and mallet and guy-rope pegs to him as to a surgeon at the operating table. It was when he had directed her to go round tightening the guy-ropes that she had difficulty with one of them and in handing over to him she stumbled over the peg, fell sprawling on to hands and knees and brought him down with her.

For a moment or two they were a laughing entanglement of legs and flailing arms, unaware, as they sorted themselves out, that they were not alone. Una knelt up, brushing down her thighs, to find Zante standing above her and looking a question towards Roland Luard.

They were both on their feet now. Una said, 'Oh—Zante!' and on hearing the name, Roland introduced himself.

Zante said, 'Yes, Petro Elmerio said you would be interested. If you had let us know you were coming over I'd have been here to meet you. I wouldn't have left my wife to come alone.' Smooth words enough, but Una blushed for their inner bite. Zante was daring to judge the rough-and-tumble he had witnessed, and she longed to tell him that it had been about the first time that he and his island would have heard her laugh aloud in spontaneous, unshadowed mirth.

Obviously missing the sting, Roland said, 'That's all right. The Professor roped me into the team at once, and I've been making myself useful ever since.'

'And enjoying yourself.' Zante's glance appraised the tent, then he said to Una, 'If Daniel can spare you, I think I'll steal you from him. The light on Teriki was fading, so I called it a day. Ready, darling, to go?'

She hesitated. 'Father wanted me to do some more photographing for him——'

'No problem. I can do it.' Roland patted his camera-case.

'Then would you?' Zante's tone took it for granted as he moved off, a hand under Una's elbow. She turned back. 'You'll come over again?' she asked Roland.

'Any time I'm wanted. I'll check with the Professor. And I'll see you both again?' If he were aware by now that he had been snubbed, he gave no sign, and Una was grateful to him.

Seated beside Zante in the car, she said, 'I suppose you found my note? I think you could have left one for me.'

'There was no point. When I left this morning, I didn't know where I'd be making for.'

'You could have said at least that you had gone painting, instead of leaving me to guess. And what—where—is Teriki?'

'It's a bay—really only a cove—facing south to Kassikona.'

'And by mentioning it you had to pretend to that young man that I knew where you were? Supposing Father or he had asked me, and I'd had to admit that I didn't know?'

'You would have had to laugh it off that I'd made you a grass widow for the day, wouldn't you? Awkward for you, but to save your own face I daresay you could have laughed convincingly enough. And if I choose, may have to again.'

Mortified and resentful, Una could not trust herself to reply, and the silence lasted until Zante remarked, 'Eager beaver, this Luard. Did Daniel welcome him?'

'Yes. He's done some digging as an amateur, and he says he's fluent in Greek.'

'There is a man among the gang who speaks and understands English,' Zante said sharply.

'Yes, well, I suppose it won't hurt to have two, and the labourers won't still be there when the actual dig starts, will they?'

'And you hope that the Luard youth will?'

Telling herself she must ignore the provocation of that, Una said, 'Naturally. And you enlisted him yourself, didn't you?'

'Only sight unseen, by proxy through his hosts.'

'And so?'

'And so, my dear, in the interests of our image, yours and mine, I hope you'll see, when you are on the site yourself, that he doesn't enjoy himself *too* extravagantly at your expense. You understand?'

'I know what you want me to understand,' Una muttered.

'Good.'

'Though I can only hope your unnecessary dog-in-the-manger warnings didn't get through to Mr Luard!'

'And I hope they did. They were meant to,' said Zante with finality.

Una had dreaded meeting Maria at dinner that night, lest her mood should have veered again to hostility. But to Una's relief she was comparatively cheerful and relaxed, as if her spirits were enjoying a similar blessed remission to that which the lifting of physical pain might have given her.

It was she who suggested to Zante that he should give a party for Una. 'Through your marrying in England, you cheated all your friends of a reception, and you should make it up to them now,' she said.

Cringing inwardly, Una sent a look of appeal to Zante. Surely he couldn't welcome such a falsity, could he?

But it seemed that he could. He answered his aunt, but his sapphire-dark eyes met and held Una's in challenge as he said, 'You have forestalled me, Maria. I was going to discuss with Una exactly that idea this evening. With a view to some time next week, I thought?'

He is not consulting me now—he is telling me, thought Una as Maria approved, 'And none too soon, if we are not to have the busybodies of Corfu wondering why you married without their blessing, and without giving them the chance to applaud your choice.' She turned to Una. 'You will let Zante have his party to show off his bride, my dear, will you not?'

Again Una silently begged Zante to spare her this shame, this desecration of the lovely word 'bride'. Without his help, which would not be hers to command, she could only make the feeble excuses of false modesty and shyness which Maria would rightly enough reject. There was nothing she could reasonably say against this gathering of Zante's friends to meet her and appraise her and to go away discussing and criticising, and all of them callously deceived ... So she agreed with as much grace as she could muster. Zante should have his way with her in this, as in everything else, though how much hostess-ship he would expect of her against this alien background she did not know. She knew nothing of Greek social customs, none of the language, and had yet to learn all the names and functions of the house staff. How, in such circumstances, was she to appear anything but gauche and naïve and counterfeit, the utter sham which Zante had made of her?

As to the practical details, she need not have worried. When she raised them with Zante he dismissed them as being no concern of hers. He would issue the invitations in both their names; nearly all the guests spoke English; the catering and even the flowers would be in the hands of Corfu firms; Una had only to look her part and make herself pleasant to her guests.

'My part as—what?' she asked rebelliously.

'As Mrs Zante Diomed, of course. What do you mean to wear?' He had ignored the bitterness as if she had not uttered it.

She mentally reviewed her wardrobe—slacks, cool dresses, a couple of simple long ones. 'I don't know. Something eveningish, I suppose.'

'Naturally—for an evening affair. You'd better go over to Athens and get something new.'

'To *Athens*?' (Athens. On the mainland. And he had said 'go over', as if he meant to send her alone.) For one wild moment of fantasy her echo of the city's name had spoken her thought—that once there, she might escape him and his island and all the humiliation they meant. She could disappear in Athens, get back to England somehow——! But in the same instant that her honesty knew, as it had done once before, that she would not take the way of physical, scurrying escape from him, she saw from her glance into his face that he knew what the tempting thought had been. But all he said was an easy, 'We'll take the car over on the ferry and fly down from Corfu. Tomorrow perhaps? Yes? Then I'll ring to make sure the steamer calls.'

It was the modern, sophisticated Athens which Una was to see that day—the city of skyscrapers and international hotels and exclusive restaurants and *haute couture* salons, in several of which Zante was welcomed as a privileged client. Escorting how many women before her? Una wondered, but knew herself to be too proud to ask.

It was he who asked to be shown the models, and he who disappointed the *vendeuses* by saying that for the moment Madame needed no design to be made for her—merely a ready-made gown for a single occasion. Yes—for a reception where, as his bride of less than a month, she was to be the hostess. And yes again, agreeing with the vendeuse and her minions, while his appraising glance raked her from head to foot—something which would bring out Madame's peculiarly English type of beauty.

Beauty! She had none, and he knew it. He was simply playing along with the chirruping flattery of these ingratiating yes-women. For her part, Una told herself, she would have preferred to go window-shopping for something strictly off-the-peg and within her budget. Or would she ...? Could any girl wilfully deny herself the once-in-a-lifetime luxury of being dressed to please the man she loved, even though he saw it only as a social exercise, and herself as the symbol to his friends of his acquisition of a wife? She ought, she supposed, to have the moral courage to let the silken whisper of one of these gowns drop to her feet and to step out of with a No! to Zante which only he would understand. *He* would know that with the gesture she was rejecting the whole cruel masquerade; the *vendeuses* would only suppose she disliked that particular model. But she could not do it, and she was in little doubt that his power with her knew she would not dare.

He would not even let her have the dress she liked best. It was a pale cerulean blue with tiny cap sleeves a softly draped bodice and a full skirt, banded above the hem with three rows of silver braid. When Zante shook his head at it, she protested, 'Why not?

It's simple and it's "my" colour. Any shade of blue always is.'

'But not this time.' He signalled her back to the dressing-room where a fitter was hovering with a rich fall of gold over her arm. 'The gold, please,' he said, and when Una had been, as she expressed it, 'poured' into the shining metallic sheath with its daringly-split skirt, the maturity of long, wrist-tight sleeves and an economy of line over hips and waist and breasts which emphasised every curve and swell of her figure, she gasped at her new image.

She stood in front of Zante, blushing against her will. 'It's too——' Old for me? Showy? Glamorous? —she had not chosen the word she wanted when he nodded a thoughtful 'Yes,' and walked slowly round her, trailing a fingertip along the nape of her neck above the high mandarin collar, in a featherlight touch which could have been that of a lover but was not.

He said Yes again, and then to the *vendeuse*, 'Tell Madame please, will you, why not the blue?'

The woman simpered. 'Ah, Kyrie Diomed, you should not make me!'

'I am asking you. Come along—explain.'

'Ah well——!' Fat beringed hands were folded across the amplitude of the black satin midriff as she turned with a coy smile to Una.

'It is because, Madame,' she said in careful, slow English, 'in Greece we say the blue, the blue of the sea, the heavenly blue is a colour only for virgins. And you, Madame, are a happy, fortunate wife!'

CHAPTER FIVE

To the gold dress were added gold kid sandals, a cobweb of an evening shawl and a gold mesh bag from the salon's boutique, and before they left Athens Zante arranged for a hairdresser to come out to the island to do Una's hair on the day of the party.

He handled the guest list himself and when the acceptances came in he passed them to Una with comments as to who the invitees were.

There were politicians, rich expatriates from several countries, Greek men of business and their wives and others whom he labelled merely as his friends.

In view of Maria's antipathy for Selene Trepano Una wondered whether he had committed the folly of inviting her, and asked him about it.

'Of course,' he said tersely. 'And her mother.'

'Oh—was that wise?' Una questioned. 'Maria——'

He frowned. 'This is my house and I invite to it whom I please,' he claimed.

'Roughshod over Maria's very understandable prejudices, if Selene did turn down Jason as heartlessly as she believes.'

'Tcha! That is just her magnification of a very ordinary jilting by a girl of a youth for whom she had no use. Maria has to justify Jason's deserting her to go to England, and so she has chosen to make Selene her scapegoat for that, whereas it is England and'—Zante paused significantly—'the enemies who destroyed him there, which are by far the deeper causes of her bitterness.'

The oblique thrust at her went home, as Una guessed he had meant it should. Ignoring it, she said, 'You really are not afraid Maria might create a scene, as she did the other night?'

He shook his head. 'I doubt it. She is too well-bred to call attention to her obsessions in my house in public. Besides, odd as it may seem, she likes Selene's mother. They are much of an age; they have both been *grandes dames* in their time and in their social circles, and they always welcome each other with some extravagance. I imagine they have to keep off the subject of Selene and Jason, but otherwise they get on well enough.'

During the days before the party an army of professionals took over the house. Lanterns and fairy lights were hung in the gardens; caterers took orders and gauged the capacity of the kitchen; there were deliveries of wine, flowers and musicians' paraphernalia, and a special sailing of the steamer was to bring over the guests from Corfu. Una hardly saw Zante, and though she was glad to escape to the site every day, when she railed against the ostentation of it all she got little sympathy from her father.

'You should be glad that Zante is proud enough of you to want to show you off to his friends,' Daniel chided in his blessed ignorance of the facts.

'He still needn't make such a public spectacle of me!' (When Zante decided she had atoned enough, would he drum her out of town with much the same sound and fury?) 'All this glamour isn't *me*. I can't live up to it, as he should know.'

'I don't suppose he expects you to, every day,' Daniel soothed. 'In fact, I know he doesn't. He loves you for what you are and were when he met you, and if this one-time operation in showiness is his way of letting people see how he prizes you, then you should let him have his way. You haven't tried to nag him out of it, I hope?'

'No.'

'Sensible girl,' approved Daniel. 'When a man of Zante's purpose means to have his way, anyone else may save their breath. For instance, look how easy he made it for me to start my Greek project here, and once he had made up his mind to marry you, didn't he sweep you off your feet?'

Una nodded. 'But I—wanted to be swept.'

'Then "want" with him in this. Don't be a sour-puss.'

She smiled ruefully. 'In other words, you are completely on Zante's side?'

'When he is in the right. What's more, daughter mine, you know in your heart that you are going to enjoy his making you Queen of the May for a night!' Daniel declared robustly.

'Am I?' If only he didn't trust Zante so implicitly! If only he knew that in duping her, Zante had duped him too. If he had had the slightest doubts of Zante's good faith, it might be easier to

disillusion him with the truth. But Zante had seen
to it that she had neither the heart nor the will for
that. He had reckoned shrewdly on her concern for
Daniel and for Maria, as he had played on her love
for him—and so far had won.

The nearer the evening of the party, the more
she viewed it with a nervous excitement which was
not, she had to admit, without a frisson of pleasure.
Her femininity was going to rise to the challenge of
looking, at Zante's demand, a different, more glamorous Una than the everyday one her mirror re-
flected. That Una, she hoped, might find the lights,
the music and other people's gaiety infectious
enough to allow her to forget the sham of it all and
to play the bride without a guilty backward look at
the no-man's-wife the real Una was.

Clytie, one of the maids, came to help her to
dress. Between them, laughing, they eased her into
the gold dress over her elaborately piled hair, and
Clytie stood back, clapping her hands and murmur-
ing *'Tee amici!'* which, after a troubled minute or
two, Una managed to translate as 'How lovely!'
then followed it with a chatter of Greek, of which
the only words Una understood were 'Kyrios
Diomed'.

Zante had dressed earlier and Una waited until
she heard the first car arriving before she went
downstairs. Zante, in dark brown velvet jacket and
pale coffee evening shirt and slacks, was in the hall,
talking to the drinks waiter, and Una paused on the
staircase, looking down at his gold-bronze head
which was her foreshortened view of him from

where she stood ... loving his looks, loving him, aching with nostalgia for the days when she had believed he loved her.

He looked up, saw her, and for one enchanted moment his eyes betrayed him to the same look of pleasure as he had often worn in those days at any unexpected sight of her. He would have followed it up with a kiss and the equivalent of Clytie's 'How lovely!' and she would have basked in the sun of loving and being loved alike.

Tonight there was again the look, but it must have been self-congratulatory for his success in glamorising her. And there was also the kiss—but formally, for her hand, as she joined him and stood at his side in readiness to greet their guests.

People came. Zante gave them her name and gave theirs to her, not expecting, she hoped, that she would remember half of them to fit to their owners when she met them again. A few of them stood out from the rest. Some extremely chic women, one or two exceptionally beautiful girls, the people who were English or American, or who spoke English well enough to put her at her ease. She would remember Dana and Petro Elmerio, Roland Luard's host and hostess, because they came with him. And she guessed that the stately lady in black with high-caste features who made it her first duty to embrace the seated Maria 'with extravagance', as Zante had put it, was Selene Trepano's aristocratic mother, for Selene was behind her with a thickset man of about forty, with jet-black eyes and fat hands, as Una noticed on shaking hands with him when

Selene adroitly avoided Maria and came straight on
to Una and Zante, whom she saluted with a kiss on
his cheek, asking Una, 'You would like that I speak
English all the evening?' and introduced her companion as her mother's cousin Florio Varani, Italian
and a film producer.

'He speaks English too. He is on vacation with us,
but he says he looks for——' She broke off. 'What is
the word you have to tell me what it means?' she appealed to Varani.

'Talent?' he offered.

'Ah yes, and when I say what is that, he says
"Beautiful girls", and so then *I* say, "Well, look at
me." '

'With a view to—what?' asked Zante sharply.

Selene seemed to have to wrestle with 'With a
view to'. Shaking her head over it, she said, 'He
could make me a star.'

'And *have* you looked at her with that idea?'
Zante demanded of Varani, who shrugged and
laughed.

'Of course I have looked at her. With her looks,
what man wouldn't?' he said with pseudo-gallantry
in fluent English. 'But I have to tell her that I am
not in the market for nubile young starlets just
now——'

'And so?' Zante cut in with an edge to his tone.

'And so, no sale, I'm afraid. Better luck next
time, baby—hm?' As Varani reached to take a play-
ful pinch of Selene's cheek, she slapped down his
hand, hissed a brief Greek word at him, and
flounced away.

The odious man—Una already thought of him so —looked after her, then laughed again. 'I'm afraid that was a rude name she called me,' he said.

'It was,' Zante confirmed shortly, then looked over and beyond him to welcome some other people. It was the snub direct, telling Una, if not Florio Varani, that to cross swords with Zante on the subject of Selene was a hazardous thing to do.

People scattered about the lovely rooms, formed groups, broke up and re-grouped in a shifting kaleidoscope of colour and talk and laughter. For Una there was scarcely a moment when she was not in demand. Whenever she stood alone, Zante seemed to appear from nowhere, bringing people to her or taking her to them. Whatever she said gained an attention to which she was not used; wherever she moved she was aware of eyes watching her. Zante had seen to it that, like a girl on her wedding day, she was the most important person there, and she would not have been human if, the adulation going to her head, she had not found it easy to make-believe that it was all true and that she really was Zante's bride in every understood way.

She took supper with Daniel and one of the Corfu lovelies and her husband, and if she needed any reward for her silence it would have been there for her in the happiness on Daniel's face when she and Zante were toasted in champagne. Afterwards, there was a move towards dancing and a demand that they take the floor alone in the first waltz.

He held out his hand to her; she took it and was swept into his arms. He held her close ... closer than he need, as if stating his possession of her against the world. During their courtship they had not danced often together, and when they had, they had been more relaxed than now.

She tensed within his hold, in consequence dancing less well than she could, but eager, too eager, to savour to the full his nearness, their bodies aligned, thigh brushing thigh, his arm about her waist a claiming, her hand in his a mute surrender.

She looked up, met his glance and looked away from what she thought she read in his eyes. A sardonic triumph—'Look how well we're playing this!'? Or congratulations on her success with his friends? Either/or, it was less than she wanted to see. There had been no promise there at all.

The seductive music swayed on. Other couples joined them on the floor and they went on dancing until Selene, passing by with Roland Luard, suddenly halted and cut in upon them with a little tap on Zante's arm. He stopped, looked for Una's permission to make the exchange, and at her nod released her. As he moved off with Selene, she laughed. '"Take what you want", they say. So I am bold—and *take*!' The other two did not hear Zante's reply.

They walked off the floor together. Roland said, 'I've hardly seen anything of you. Have you been in the gardens yet? No? Then shall we——?'

The gardens were a dark, dappled-with-light scented fairyland. They wandered along the paths, meeting or avoiding other strolling couples, and at last were isolated on a seat at the parapet overlooking the drop below.

Roland asked solicitously, 'You won't be cold? Would you like me to bring you a drink?'

'Presently. Not now.' In a way it was good to be brought down to earth by the everyday sanity of Roland, associating him as she did with work, since he was so often at the site when she was that she wondered what time he could be giving to his own project.

He asked her when Daniel planned to begin excavating for finds.

'In a week or two,' she said.

'And what, principally, shall we be looking for?'

She laughed. 'Anything and everything, and perhaps for days on end, finding nothing. An archaeologist's patience has to be infinite. But here Father's day will be made when he or someone comes up with a trace of something Egyptian—a bronze or fragments of pottery or some ivory.'

'Because that will show the Greek-Egyptian trade worked both ways?'

'Well, we know it did between the mainland and the bigger islands like Crete and Samos. But evidence on as small an island as this would be very important.'

Roland said, 'Yes, so I gathered from the Professor. You know, you're such an archaeologist yourself that I wonder one of your father's colleagues didn't spot the kindred soul in you, and snap you up and marry you.'

'They were mostly married men of Father's age or students who were too young for me. Not a chance!' Una laughed.

'And then your husband came along, after which there was never a chance for anything else?'

'Not really.'

Roland nodded. 'Pretty obvious—worse luck for all the men here tonight who would give their right hands to be in his place!'

'But not because of me.'

'What else than you? He worships you, and no wonder. Although—' Roland turned in his seat and looked at her, 'I hadn't realised myself until tonight just how beautiful you are, d'you know?'

She forced a laugh at that. 'It's a trick of the light,' she said.

'I only wish it were——' He left the low intensity of that to a silence which might have led to anything, had she been willing or he been bolder. But after a minute or two he broke it himself with a rueful, 'Don't mind me. Just bemoaning my being too late behind a certain Zante Diomed, that's all!' And then, easing the tension, for which she was grateful to him, 'Will you have a drink now? Would you stay here, if I went for one?'

'Of course.' She told him her choice, then stopped him as he was about to leave. 'And Roland—my shawl? I believe I left it on the piano in the salon. A lacy, cream thing. I think I'd like it now.'

When he had gone, she drew a long, relieved breath that he hadn't let the magic of the evening spoil their friendship with a flirtation which they both knew could lead to nothing. He liked her, she knew, and she liked him, but it was a daytime, down-to-earth—on the site, literally!—companion-ship in which the to-and-fro of flirtation had no part. She smiled into the darkness. Bless you, she told the absent Roland, for knowing it! And then, with a stab of pain, *Bless you too, for believing so hard that Zante loves me, that for one mad moment you had me hoping and half-believing you were right.*

There were footsteps on the path behind her, and she turned, expecting Roland. But it was the Italian, Florio Varani, strolling alone. As his hostess she had to acknowledge him, and he took her chilly smile as an invitation to sit beside her.

She got up and went to lean on the parapet. He followed, standing elbow to elbow with her. 'This is more than I'd hoped for—to find you alone,' he said in a thick, ingratiating voice. 'Just taking the night air? No escort? Nor an infatuated bride-groom, reluctant to allow you out of his sight? But no, of course—you were able to escape *him*, oc-cupied as he is for the moment with his little model, my fiery young cousin!'

'I have an escort. He's bringing some drinks,' Una said coldly, and then, 'I'm so glad if Zante is giving Selene a good time. He's very fond of her, I know. And if I may say so, Signor Varani, she hardly deserved the rather cheap remarks I heard you make at her expense in front of Zante and me.'

'Pff!' he scoffed. 'She asked for all I said. Asks all the time, with her body and her eyes and everything she has which she thinks will appeal to men. As it may, to callow *ragazzi* of her own age, or to professionals like your husband, for whom she is only a figure and a face he has chosen to paint—though no doubt occasionally sweet to the taste also——'

At Una's sharp-drawn breath, 'I shock you, Signora?' he peered into her face to ask.

'You—disgust me.'

'Because I tell the truth—that artist types like your husband take to themselves the right to pick a little here, a little there, of the freely offered fruit, without a thought of betrayal of their lovely wives, whom they married, as I am sure Signor Diomed married you for quite other qualities—for your gravity, for an air of untouched virginity which you still retain, for your suggestion of hidden depths— these are the things which inflame a man to real passion, Signora. As ... they ... inflame ... me——'

The last words were ground from between his teeth, and before she could resist him, his arms were about her and his hot bulbous lips were upon her unresponsive mouth. She struggled with him wordlessly, but though he was no taller than she, his thick arms were strong and his lustful kisses were random on hair, cheeks and jawline.

With one hand he pinioned her, while his other went to fumble at the buttons of the upstanding collar of her gown. One by one he forced them from their frogged loops, and horrified by the outcome, should he free them all to the cleavage of her breasts, Una tried a desperate tactic. Momentarily she lowered her taut-held shoulders, loosened the fists which were thrusting at his chest, and relaxed with a pseudo-willingness in his arms—not long enough to deceive him into thinking she had surrendered, but as a preliminary to a prodigious effort to set herself free.

But in the moment before she braced herself to that, she looked beyond his shoulder to see that they were no longer alone.

Roland, thank God! But it was not Roland Luard who stood watching. It was Zante, a silhouette of silent menace which boded the worst. But for the man Varani, surely? He couldn't— *couldn't* be blaming her!

Whether or not, she could not tell as she stood, fingering her open collar, and Varani, aware now that they were not alone, released her, panting and straightening his tie and jacket, while Zante stood there, still saying nothing.

An unbidden sob of anger caught in her throat. 'I——' she began, but other people were there by then—Roland, carrying her shawl, followed by a waiter with their drinks on a salver. Then Zante, regardless of whether or not Roland was concerned in the scene, ordered him peremptorily, 'Take my wife back to the house, will you, please?' and waited while Roland draped the shawl about Una's shoulders and gestured the waiter to turn back on his tracks.

With a hand beneath her elbow, he made his apologies. 'Sorry I was so long,' he said. 'But when I went to get your shawl some woman had dropped her ring just there and we couldn't but help to find it.' He bent to look into her ravaged face. 'But what happened?'

They had halted outside the lighted salon. 'Not your fault,' she told him. 'It was that Italian—a relative of Selene Trepano's. He joined me while I was waiting for you, and he—made a heavy pass. And Zante came down the garden and saw him ... saw us, just before you arrived.'

'The swine! Let's hope he's being dealt with.'

'Yes, but—— Look, he is a guest, and if he turned ugly, it would make an awful scandal. I suppose you wouldn't go back and see what's happening, would you?' Una pleaded.

'Try to get them to cool it? Of course.' Roland turned. 'You go in and do your hostess stuff, and I'll come back and report.' He took his glass from the waiter's tray and drained it. Una carried hers into the house and found a seat half hidden by a bank of palms, from which she could pretend to watch the dancing.

When Roland returned Zante came with him. She saw them part with a brief nod, and Roland came over to her. Zante went on his way.

'Well?' she questioned. 'What happened? Where is Signor Varani?'

Roland said, 'Gone to the men's room to clean up his bloodied nose, I shouldn't wonder. After that, I doubt if he'll reappear. He'll probably find his way down to one of the tavernas and wait for the return steamer there. Anyway, when I got there, your husband had him by his bunched shirt and tie, and when Varani saw me, he sort of choked, "So why blame me? *He* had her first—I saw them"—meaning us, you see.'

Una's fingers flew to her mouth. 'Oh *no!*' she breathed.

'His very words. Upon which Zante punched him, but not too hard, because he was able to come up again with——' Roland checked. 'Oh no, I'm not going to repeat that, d'you mind?'

'What was it?' she urged. 'Please—you must tell me!'

But he was adamant. 'No,' he said. 'It was too filthy. Anyway, then Zante really hit him—on the jaw, and we left him staggering back from the parapet where he'd slumped.'

'You left him hurt?'

'Not so badly that he couldn't walk. I heard him blundering up the path some way behind us. There's a cloaks man, isn't there? Let *him* clean him up.'

'And Zante—with you?'

'Said nothing but "Forget it", when I explained that the reptile was lying—that you and I were only sitting out a dance and going to have a drink. He was probably too mad to trust himself to be civil—I don't hold it against him.'

'You don't think——? I mean, he couldn't blame me, could he?' Una appealed pitifully.

'Blame you? For what, for heaven's sake?'

'For whatever it was that Varani accused me of, that you won't tell me.'

'Nor will I. Anyway, it wasn't anything about you—in particular,' Roland added uncomfortably. 'It was—well, an ugly crack that set Zante on fire, that's all.' He pointed to her glass. 'Let me get you a brandy in that, and you'll feel a new woman.'

She shook her head. 'No. I'll go and freshen up— after that mauling. I'm not looking forward to meeting Zante too soon, but we mustn't spoil the evening for everyone else.'

The evening was not spoiled if the euphoria of the departing guests an hour or two later was any measure of the enjoyment they claimed to have had. Only one contretemps arose when the last of the Corfu party were on their way out. Then Signor Varani was noticed to be missing, and Zante volunteered blandly that he had needed air and had probably gone ahead alone to the quays.

'Air? *Air*?' snapped Selene. 'He has taken our hired car and hasn't sent it back!'

'Whose? Yours and your mother's? That's all right. I'll drive you down myself,' Zante offered. The hall had emptied now, and he turned to Una. 'Go to bed,' he told her. 'If you are asleep, I won't disturb you.'

She managed a smile for him. 'I shan't be,' she said. 'When you come back—please? I'd—like to talk about the party.'

She had guessed he meant to come, but she had had to make certain. She could not sleep until she knew what Zante had made of the degrading scene; hear him tell her he knew she hadn't invited it. He had told Roland, 'Forget it'. So could she hope he would say the same to her?

She hadn't to wait longer than she expected to

hear him come up, but he went through to his own room from the corridor. That heartened her. If he were as angry as he had looked when he had come upon her in the Italian's arms, he would have wasted no time in telling her so. Relaxing a little, she drew the pins out of her hair and began to brush it.

When he came in through the connecting door, she saw in the mirror that he had undressed. Hands in the pockets of his short robe, he stood looking at her reflection from across the room, then came over and took the brush from her. 'I told you to go to bed,' he said. 'Or were you thinking of sitting up in your party gear all night?'

'Of course not. I was waiting for you.' Slowly she began to unbutton her dress from the throat downward, until he commented, 'Making rather heavy weather of the job, aren't you? Not so eager as you were earlier tonight?'

Her fingers stilled. 'You—you didn't think I was —*willing*?' she faltered.

'To the onlooker you seemed reasonably pliant— both hands spread on manly chest; playing the reluctant nymph, but only a matter of time until he was given permission to complete the operation— hm?'

She drew a long breath of utter despair. 'So you did think I was willing, that I could have helped myself?'

'You weren't exactly resisting, were you? And in a few more minutes he would have uncovered all he wanted——'

'He would *not*! I knew he was too strong for me, so I relaxed to deceive him——'

'Frustrating, you hoped, your second attempted ravishment of the evening?'

'My second? What do you mean?' But she knew. He had believed Varani's accusation of Roland, and listened to Roland's explanation of how she had come to be at Varani's mercy. He hadn't believed her; he hadn't believed Roland. Dear God, perhaps he thought Roland and Varani had been in it together to seduce her! Had taken turns ... And Zante, impelled by no forgivable jealousy of her, had still despised her enough to make her suffer to the hilt. She answered her own question for him.

'You're suggesting that I went out there with them both?' she asked.

'Or one after the other—it makes no odds. In quick succession, anyway.'

'And if I'm supposed to have encouraged Varani, why did you hit him, as Roland says you did? Since you care nothing for me yourself, I wonder you didn't wish him more power to his elbow, and hit me instead?'

Zante looked down at her beneath hooded lids. 'A good question, as you say in England,' he drawled. 'The answer being that there are other ways of punishing a woman than resorting to fisticuffs, and I hit Varani because he put the situation rather *too* crudely for my taste.'

Recollection flashed. The thing Roland had refused to repeat! 'What was it he said?' she asked. 'Something scurrilous about me?'

Zante said, as Roland had done, 'Not naming you, but making himself understood very well indeed. He said, "Put a couple of stallions in a field, with a filly in heat on the far side of the hedge, and what do you expect?" Upon which I hit him a second time, and he stayed hit.'

'That—that's horrible!' Una gasped.

'Gutter language to describe the fellow's impression that you were thirsting for what any male could do for you, given invitation. As for why I hit him, do you suppose'—Zante gripped her upper arm and shook it—'do you suppose I care for the story to get around that Mrs Zante Diomed is eager and easy for any stud who likes to stake a claim? Well, do you?' he demanded through gritted teeth. '*Do* you?'

'No. Because it had to be that,' she said stonily. 'You didn't lash out from any jealous defence of me, but because the name of Zante Diomed mustn't be sullied *through* me. Caesar's wife, in fact ... above suspicion. Except that I'm—no wife. That's the difference.'

'And a difference which you probably think entitles you to a roving eye for any chance that offers. *But* a difference which I can wipe out, I'd remind you, whenever I choose.'

'But you won't choose. It suits your purpose to keep me as I am. And besides, I've warned you, I wouldn't let you,' she defied him.

'And I shouldn't be too sure of that if I were you,' he said. 'Either that I may not "choose" when it suits me, or that you could thwart me if and when it does. Come here——'

The order was superfluous, since he still held her by the arm. But his leverage upon it brought her round to face him, and with his other hand he pulled her so tightly to him that every contour of her body, thigh, hip, breast, shoulder was aligned to the hard resistance of his.

They were within a few paces of her bed and he propelled her backwards towards it, pressing her down when she could sit, and, sitting askew beside her, began calmly and methodically to push down her half-opened dress over her shoulders and to strip it from the rest of her body, kicking it carelessly aside. The straps of her slip and bra went next, and then he had lifted her legs on to the bed and was looking at her ... touching her in a way which sent a flame of desire racing through her veins.

He said in a new, strange voice, 'You see—you aren't fighting me off. What did I tell you once—that the body sometimes imposes its own will, as yours is doing now. You would like to resist but you can't. You've been roused, and you need——' He broke off and lowered his body to rest with controlled weight upon hers, warm flesh to warm flesh, moulding and clinging, while his lips sought and found hers in a hot, bruising demand to which every fibre within her responded.

If only it were real. If only he desperately wanted her, as she wanted him! Hoping, longing to believe that it was so, and that his own body's will was driving him to admit that he had passion for her, if not any affection, because she would settle for his physical need of her if she had to, she moved with a little cry that was almost a purr of delight. But at his response to it, an urgent searching with his hands, while he kept her mouth imprisoned beneath his, revulsion suddenly caught at her throat in a surge that was almost physically sickening.

He didn't want her. He couldn't, so swiftly upon anger, his suspicions of her. He was only showing her with a kind of male braggadocio that he could rouse her, could take her if he wanted to—banking on the love she had shown him too readily in the past, to take her or to reject her as he chose. As, at the peak of her gift of herself, he probably meant to reject her. He had done it once before, and could again, for all his seeming abandonment now.

At the thought she went cold, calculating a move which would reject him first. Nothing overt, like turning from him, protesting. No, pretending modesty or shyness—she had responded too far in passion for that. Her only weapon was scorn, a ridicule that should slap him in the face——

She thrust the back of her hand beneath his chin, levering it backward, so that he had to lift his head.

'I'm surprised that you're content to be the *third* stallion in line,' she said—and waited.

The exploring hands stilled. The pressure of his body against hers lightened. Something changed in the deep blue eyes into which she stared, turning them as grey as an iced-over pool—opaque, unfathomable, remote. He flung her hand away, then took her by that wrist and jerked her upright. He straightened and stood over her, slung his robe about his shoulders and thrust his hands deep into its pockets.

To keep them from going murderously to her throat? she wondered, panic-stricken. But he made no move, said nothing, and after a minute or two left her crouched, head bowed in hands in horror that she could be the object of such glacial, controlled fury as her deliberate taunt had provoked.

What had she done?

CHAPTER SIX

SOMEHOW she dragged herself into bed. Somehow she fitfully slept. The sun, when it waked her finally, seemed a menace, an affront. The night had been her refuge from Zante's anger and now that had gone.

Thought came back. Fear. In the big alien bed her body curled instinctively into the defensive foetal position as she recalled the moment of dread she had known when she guessed that he had had to clench his fists against the impulse to do her violence. At the time she had calculated her flung insult as self-protection from his arrogated claim to dominate her body without any tenderness for her. But if his pride—for it was *only* his pride that she could touch on the raw!—were more vulnerable than she thought it, then she had gone too far, and perhaps he had had the right to go berserk.

But he had not. He had simply brushed her aside as if she were a piece of dusty trash in his path, subjected her to that unreadable blind stare and left her to the lonely silence she had invited; to the same rejection as she had foreseen and had tried to forestall.

Now, she wondered, what was it all going to mean to mean to the future or his revenge? On the surface, perhaps nothing, since his compulsion upon

her to act out the charade of normal, happy re-
lations *was* his revenge. But beneath the veneer of
lasting honeymoon, what might he be planning as
an extra punishment? She was no patient Griselda,
and she was afraid for a love that might be able to
take just so much breaking of its spirit and no more.

Both he and Maria were at the breakfast-table before her, and the tone between them all was falsely
normal as they inevitably talked 'party' and the success it seemed to have been.

Una knew that, late night or no on the evening
before, Daniel would be on the site as usual, and in
order to escape the clearing up of the party debris
in which Maria assured her they would both be
more hindrance than help, she meant to join him.
When she said so, Zante surprised her by offering,
'I'll drive you over, and have a day there myself.'

To date he had confined his early offer of help to
supplying labour and the promise of volunteer en-
thusiasts, and had visited the site only briefly. But
during the next several days he went to it regularly
with her, causing her to wonder cynically whether
his object was to police her contacts with Roland.
But though they would all lunch alfresco together,
he worked mostly in Daniel's company, while she
and Roland paired off into the partnership of two
in which Daniel liked his teams to work when the
actual dig began.

He had rushed the preliminary work along, demanding more of himself than Una thought he
should, going to the site soon after dawn and staying

on for as long as the evening light lasted. But she understood his having made September the deadline for closing down the project if they had made no significant finds before then. There would be no point in keeping the workings open through the torrential winter rains of the region if there were little prospect of any better success in the spring.

September—after which, if circumstances sent Daniel home empty-handed, Zante would no longer have any leverage upon her silence, thought Una, yet she could not have said whether the time between then and now seemed too long or too short.

At last, his huts built, his exploratory trenches dug to his working plans, Daniel called a kind of dress rehearsal of his volunteers, lining them up at the stores hut for the issue of the trowels, the sieves, the brush-and-dustpans and sorting bags which were the tools of their trade, and noting who would partner whom on the sections to which each partnership was allotted. The dig proper would begin the next day.

Una knew that Zante had done very little painting while he had shared Daniel's intensive work on the site, and she hardly expected him to join the dig. But on that first morning he had two surprises in store for her. He loaded painting gear on to the car, saying he meant some time to paint the activity on the site, and he made a detour to the harbour to pick up Selene.

'Is she interested in archaeology?' Una asked as they waited for her boat to careen up to the jetty.

'So-so. Anyway, of an age to try any new experience,' Zante replied as she moored and they saw that she had a passenger along—Roland.

'He waits for the steamer. I ask him if he comes to Erikona, so I bring him,' she explained, and pirouetted in front of Zante. 'I am well dressed for the—what do you call it—the dig?' she asked him.

He looked over her slim figure in its trim sailor suit. 'You could have added boots and a pair of thick knee-pads with advantage. But you'll learn,' he said.

'You? You have ugly things like boots and pads for the knees?' she asked Una as they all got into the car.

'On the site,' Una told her.

'And you are clever, Zante says. You know all about this treasure we hunt?'

That showed they had discussed her. When? Una wondered jealously. 'Very far from "all",' she said, her tone short.

Selene observed next, 'My fat cousin of my mother, the toad—you make the big impression on him. He thinks you are well finished, chic and have the deep passions, he says.'

Una glanced at Zante's granite profile. 'Really?' she said.

'But from the party you give he comes back with the eye all black and the middle'—Selene pressed her diaphragm—'very pained. So someone does not like that he finds you well finished and chic, and punishes him for saying so, though he does not say who.'

There was a silence which Una wondered if

Zante and Roland found as uncomfortable as she did. Zante asked, 'Is Signor Varani still with you at the *palazzo*?'

Selene shook her head. 'No, he has gone back to Italy, mourning that he has found no talent in Greece.' She snatched the kerchief from her lovely russet hair and shook it back into the wind. 'But if he will not take a second look at a girl like me, what does he expect?' she demanded of her audience.

'You should be thankful you didn't interest him.' Zante answered the question. 'If women of deep passion are his fancy, he's not the type for you.'

Plaintively, 'He might have made me a star!'

'And if he had tried by the dubious method of the casting couch, he'd have to answer to me,' Zante snapped.

Selene frowned. 'Casting couch? What is that in Greek?'

He translated, adding an explanation at which she blushed and brightened, From the back seat of the car she leaned forward to stroke his shoulder. 'Nice Zante,' she purred praise of him. 'If toad-cousin tried to make love to me, you are telling, even in front of your wife, that you would be jealous? You might hit him again—for me?'

'Who said I hit him the first time?' Zante parried.

She spread her hands in a Latin gesture. 'But it is clear! He discovers that your wife has the deep passions. And so—you are jealous and you give him the black eye!'

'Well, you can forget the jealousy *and* the hitting in your case, my dear.'

'But you said he must answer to you! You would protect me from him!'

'I'd do my best. But as the English say, there are more ways of killing a cat——'

'Cat! Cats! We do not speak of killing cats!' Selene's bewilderment squeaked.

'No matter. Forget that too. And also that I am "telling" anything in front of Una, except that I'm not seeing you get into the hands of a type like Varani through your own silly vanity. You understand?'

She nodded and shrugged back into her seat. 'Now you *try* to be unkind,' she pouted, but when they reached the site she pranced along at his side, leaving Una and Roland to cross it together.

Roland commented, 'Refreshing little witch, isn't she?'

'An embarrassingly outspoken one.'

'Yes, well, she's the type who has to say everything she thinks. You meet 'em all the time. No doubt at all in her mind that Zante hit Varani for jealousy of you, and she wouldn't mind a share in the same kind of limelight. So she claims it, and takes umbrage when he snubs her. One wonders,' Roland added thoughtfully, 'what she thought their relationship was before he married you.'

Una left him to wonder. For herself, she knew she cared more what was Zante's involvement with Selene than for Selene's hopes of him. For one thing, his brusquerie with the girl didn't deceive her at all. Zante was the type who *didn't* say everything he was thinking, as she knew to her own bitter cost.

' "All was bustle and confusion",' Roland quoted with a laugh as they gathered at the stores hut for Daniel's briefing on their allotted sections. They dispersed to them, Selene claiming Zante as her partner when Roland assumed that Una would continue to be his. They arranged their gear and settled down to the work of scrape, shovel, sift, examine and discard, usually without reward.

A relentless sun poured down on earnestly bent heads, backbones protested, knees stiffened and hands yearned for the comfort of soap and water. A wag on a nearby section grumbled, 'I feel like that feller who was set to clean out the Augean stables!' and Roland questioned wistfully. 'D'you suppose that panning for gold or diamonds is any more rewarding than this lark—or less?'

Nothing of significance was found that day. A geiger counter unearthed some metal, and some shards of pottery which showed up were bagged and taken for Daniel's inspection. But they were all comparatively modern and were discarded, among them a promising piece of chain-store earthenware, of which the amateur finders had cherished high hopes.

At the end of a week the same wag was heard to remark, 'It must be hope as keeps us going!' and over the weekend Daniel switched the range of search to a different area. That yielded some speci-

mens worth photographing and listing. But they
were very fragmented and all of Grecian origin.
There was nothing which pointed to any early
trading between Erikona and any country over-
seas.

Daniel lost no hope, but his amateur helpers lost
some of their interest. Selene was one of the laggards
who often defected, and when she did report for
duty, she proved more decorative than useful. She
made blatant bids for Zante's attention and made a
third in Una's and Roland's partnership, though
more for chat than for work. Roland was more tol-
erant of her than Una was. 'She has a butterfly mind
like a kitten's. But she is rather engaging—so incredibly young,' he said of her indulgently.

'Though not so young that she doesn't know exactly what she wants and how to get it,' retorted
Una, and knew she had sounded tart by the ques-
tioning look he sent her in reply.

Daniel of course was always there, even on the
swelteringly hot day when, having had to put his
hired car in dock, he had trudged up to the site on
foot.

'Why on earth didn't you ring the house, and I'd
have picked you up when I collected Selene?' Zante
blamed him. But Daniel hadn't thought of that, or
so he said, though Una suspected he hadn't wanted
to give Zante the trouble.

He chose to stay on after the other helpers had
left, so Zante, Una and Selene stayed with him.
Roland had had to cry off that day, having to go
over to the mainland on his own project. Una

worked on with Daniel, cataloguing the finds of the day in the admin hut; Selene sunbathed outside and Zante took time out to work on his canvas of the site.

Earlier, when she had watched its first tentative lines emerge, Una had asked, 'What do you mean to call it?'

'*Search*, I thought,' he had said.

'Father would like it to be *Discovery*.'

'And so it may be. Though which of your English writers has said that it's better to travel hopefully than to arrive?'

'Robert Louis Stevenson, I think. You mean you are convinced Father is enjoying the searching as much as——?'

'Well, aren't you?'

'Yes. He always has,' she had agreed, and had felt a brief glow of gratitude that in this at least she and Zante were of one mind.

She stood at the open door of the hut, waiting for Daniel to have some more specimens ready for her. Zante was away, near the perimeter fence. Eyes shut, Selene lay like a sleek young animal. Behind Una in the hut there was an odd raucous sound. She turned quickly. At his bench, head upon arms, half-slipped from his chair, Daniel was motionless, except for a twitching jerk of his left elbow which spoke of agony.

'Father!' She ran to him, thrust him back on to the chair and tried to lift his head. But either he resisted or he could not help her, and she lowered it gently again. This she had seen before. She had

been there, in Egypt, when he had had his second
heart attack ... Leaving him, she ran to the door,
called urgently to Selene and pointed.

'Zante! Quick—bring him! My father——'

Selene rolled over and sat up, open-mouthed.
'You want——?'

'*Zante*. Fetch him!' Una's tone was so urgent
that Selene scrambled up and ran. Una went back
to Daniel and was kneeling by him when Zante
came to take him by the shoulders and to support
him against his own body.

'You've seen this before?' he asked Una.

'This sudden collapse—yes.'

'Professor? Daniel——?' Zante urged gently. But
though Daniel was conscious, he could not reply.
His effort was only a wordless moan.

Still holding him, Zante turned to Selene and
spoke to her in Greek up to a point where she
frowned and shook her head. His face darkened
and he repeated his words exactly, waited for her
reaction and when none came, continued to give
her what sounded like an order. She turned and left
the hut and a few minutes later she drove off the
site in Zante's car.

'Where have you sent her?' Una asked.

'First to the house, where she didn't want to go,
for fear of Maria.'

'But you made her?'

'Of course. She will tell them to have a bed made
ready for your father; then she will send Giorgio
back here with the car and borrow his runabout
to take her down to the quay. That crock of a speed-

boat of hers is fast, and the quickest way to get a doctor out from Corfu is for her to bring one back with her. With luck he could be here in an hour and a half, and we'll have you safely tucked into bed by then, eh, my friend?' Zante finished, addressing Daniel, who responded with a weary lift of his eyelids.

Zante gave more orders. 'Clear that bench,' he told Una. 'We'll make him comfortable there. Does he carry any medication with him?'

'He used to, after his last attack, but that was more than a year ago, and I don't think he has anything with him now.'

Together they laid Daniel on an improvised bed of plastic sheeting with a rolled tarpaulin for a pillow. Zante said, 'If Selene did as she was told, Giorgio can't be long now,' and went to the door of the hut to watch for him. Una stayed at Daniel's side. holding his hand, remembering how, in very similar circumstances in Egypt, she had had to cope alone until help arrived. There had been no Zante to take charge and to issue orders which people didn't dare to disobey. That was the car returning now, she thought as Zante stepped outside. Selene, however reluctantly, had done as she was told.

To love Zante blindly was one thing, but to think of him as someone to lean upon in trouble was Una's new experience in those first critical days of Daniel's illness.

Doctor Zopos, Maria's own medical man, had manfully survived his ordeal at Selena's hands, but

had been grateful to accept Zante's invitation to
stay overnight and to return to Corfu by more
orthodox means. In emergencies he could command
a helicopter; between them, he and Zante had organised this to pick up him and Daniel, and for
Daniel to be transferred with an attendant nurse
to the Athens plane for several days of intensive care
in a city hospital.

Less than twenty-four hours after Daniel's collapse, Zante and Una had seen him off from Erikona's one tiny plateau which the helicopter could
use, and as they watched it away Zante had said,

'You'd like to follow and be with him, I daresay?'

'Could I?'

'We'll go over and stay at the Theseus Palace,
which is within five minutes' walk of the hospital.'

'You would go too?'

'Of course.'

To which, for all her dependence on him, she had
retorted, 'You don't have to police me everywhere
I go, you know, as if you were afraid I shall run
away!' but was reduced to impotent silence by his
quiet,

'I'm not afraid. For I daresay you know as well as
I do that there are some things you can't escape by
running away—a guilty conscience being one of
them.'

And so that evening, having permission to pay a
short visit to a much sedated Daniel, Una went
straight to the hospital, leaving Zante to make their
booking at the hotel. When she returned her bell-

boy was given her key, showing that Zante was out, and she was swept by the obsequious child up to the second floor and into a suite of a sitting-room and a large bedroom, the dominant piece of furniture an ornate four-poster bed, not much smaller than that in her room at the White House. There was no other sleeping provision at all.

Una glanced at the door number and at the key the boy handed over.

'Are you sure Kyrios Diomed ordered this apartment?' she asked him.

He beamed. 'But yes. I bring him to mount and and see for himself,' he replied in tourist-learned English, and having to believe him, as she knew that in most foreign hotels clients were encouraged to inspect their rooms before booking, she tipped him and sent him away.

She looked at the bed and at the general luxury of the suite, wondering at Zante's intention. Surely in a hotel of this size there must be some single rooms or some simple, two-bedroom suites he could have ordered? Or was the Kyrios Diomed's standing so exalted, even here in Athens, that even for a two or three nights' emergency stay, it had to be allotted the utmost in luxury? Her curiosity was so whetted as to whether or not he had been given any choice that when she had bathed and changed into a dinner-dress, she resorted to guile to find out.

She rang Reception on the room telephone, gave her number and asked if there were any two-bedroom apartments available. At this there was a slightly stunned silence before the 'Yes' and then the question: 'Kyrios Diomed wishes to change his suite?'

'No. No—he, we find it quite satisfactory,' she lied, adding to the polite 'And so——?' of the reply, 'It was just that we expect friends may be arriving with requirements of that sort,' and rang off, torn between the petty triumph of having been right, and guilt over her spying on Zante. The latter was so strong that she knew she would be driven to confess it to him.

On her way along the corridor to the lift, she met him coming from it, and turned back with him, giving him the key. He opened the door and stood aside for her to go in.

'This will suit us?' he asked.

'I gather it suited *you*,' she replied tautly.

'But not you? Would you like to change it?'

'Reception asked that. I rang them to ask if they had anything else.'

'Why?'

'To see if they'd been able to give you any choice when you booked in.'

'They could and did—probably twin-bedded hovels on the top floor, just short of the staff quarters. I didn't pursue the matter.' He strolled into the bedroom. Nodding at the bed, 'I gather it is the promise—or the threat—of the intimacy of that which is at the root of your objection?'

'When you must have known that I at least was expecting something more—private, yes,' she said.

'Whereas I prefer the treatment they offer to

Eastern potentates who, I gather, favour the intimacy of the double bed. But I daresay we can come to terms as to which of us sleeps on the floor or curls up in a chair for the night.'

She shrank from the mockery in his tone and turned away. 'I've already changed. Shall I wait for you in the residents' lounge?' she asked.

'Do,' he agreed.

At dinner he told her he had been calling on Helena Limos, a wealthy art patron to whom he had introduced Una at their party. 'She was At Home, giving one of her "Tuesdays", and she almost literally fell upon my neck,' he said.

'Why?'

'Because she had booked a gallery for one of her young protégés who can't keep the date, and to Helena, rich as she is, waste is one of the major crimes. Besides, she enjoys the publicity for herself as generous sponsor. So she wanted to persuade me to fill the vacuum with a showing of my own stuff.'

'And will you?'

'If I find I can make a reasonable collection.' He changed the subject to ask how she had found and left Daniel.

She told him, adding that she had been given hope he might be able to leave hospital after a few more days' observation.

'When he could come back with us?'

'Yes, but of course not to work on the site.'

'Nor to go back to his lodgings. He must spend his convalescence at the White House.'

'Oh——' Una looked at the prospect in blank

dismay, then said, 'No, that's not possible. He can't do that.'

'Why not?'

'Because—oh, you must see why!' she appealed. 'Because, when he can get about again, he would know ... he would guess——'

'That we don't share the conjugal suite? Then we shall have to, for appearances' sake, just as here——'

'*No!* He must stay in hospital until he's well enough to travel, and then I must take him back to England.'

'Force him to abandon the dig? You will do nothing of the kind!' Zante ruled.

'But he can't work there now, and he's already had to abandon it.'

'For the time being. But it could open again under a deputy.'

'And who could deputise for him?'

'I should offer myself as general foreman, with you as my aide on technicalities, and with your father in the background as a kind of elder statesman until he can take back the reins or calls a halt for other reasons, such as the site's having yielded nothing by the end of the season.' Zante paused, his eyes narrowing on her shrewdly. 'I wonder,' he said, his tone falsely bland, 'whether your anxiety to whip Daniel straight back to England has as much to do with his welfare as you see it as it has with the opportunity it offers of an escape for yourself? A fair question—would you say?'

She flushed with chagrin. 'It's *not* fair, and you

know it!' she challenged, though knowing in her heart that the devious thought *had* flashed—*If I can take Father home for this good reason, then he needn't learn the truth. Or not yet. Not until——* But the thought had gone no further. Beyond that 'not until' stretched a desert of possibilities which she did not want to explore.

She had heard Zante's disbelieving 'Do I?' in answer to her outburst, but she ignored it. She objected, 'You can't give all your time to overseeing the site. Your painting—— This exhibition——'

'Needn't be an obstacle. It will only be a one-day affair, and I probably have enough canvases on hand to fill it to Helena's satisfaction. No,' he decided, 'you will not ship Daniel back to England for any reason—for *any* reason, you understand?— other than that he wants to go.'

'And supposing he does?'

'Then he will decide so for himself. Though, knowing his dedication, do you think it's likely?'

Una did not answer. Zante had won, as he always did and knew he could. There wasn't any doubt that, given the choice and the permission of his doctors, Daniel would elect to stay. Which meant that she would stay too.

When they left the dining-room Zante strolled out on to the portico beyond the main doors, open to the gentle Attic night. Una went to stand at his side.

'There is a moon,' he said.

'Yes.'

'And the Parthenon should be seen at dawn or by

moonlight.' With a touch on her elbow he turned her about. 'Go and get a wrap and we'll go up there by taxi.'

Una was to remember the rest of that night as both a near-summit of hope and a near-zero of despair.

They had left their taxi at the foot of the rock base, smoothed by millions of treading feet, which climbed gradually to the ruins of the great Doric temple which from the height of its plateau dominated both the huddle of the city and the whole of the Athenian plain.

The moonlight lay slantwise across the columns of the façade before which they stood at gaze, silent and awed by the age and the tragic beauty of all that remained of Athene's temple after nearly two thousand five hundred years. There were other people there, but they too were silent or whispering, and Una found herself doubting whether even the daytime tourists dared to do other than to stand and stare, at least for a while before their cameras began to click and their guides launched upon their historical patter.

Zante had taken her hand to help her across the glass-smooth slope of the rocks, and he still held it when they halted between the columns, viewing the vista of the interior, roofless now and bare of the sculptures which once had honoured the goddess but which, over the centuries, had been vandalised by war or taken elsewhere in the world.

'There is an Athene in the Athens museum, and a lot of the statues went to England,' Zante said.

Una nodded. 'Yes, the Elgin marbles. I have seen them.'

'And now you are seeing their original home.' He had released her hand to point, but unnecessarily he took it again. 'The two lesser temples, the Erechtheum and the Athene Niki, which has been restored with the original stone. We'll go across to them.'

She had not felt so at ease with him since they had swum together. Once she had stirred her hand in his to indicate that if to touch her was tiresome, she had no need of his help. But he had continued to hold it companionably, seeming to make a friend of her for the time being, wanting to share with her, as with a friend, the ineffable beauty of the place.

Supposing ... supposing he was beginning to soften towards her? To forgive her for the callous sin of which he thought her guilty? Supposing this night, this sharing were to mark their tentative approach to each other ... a first groping which began with the gentle contact of the holding of hands and the exchange of talk which for once had neither threat nor recoil nor false bonhomie for the benefit of onlookers, as an undercurrent to it? That might be the beginning of peace between them, of tolerance on Zante's side, if not of love.

They paused on their way down from the rock to look out over the lights of the city, and the dark expanse beyond which was the sea.

'Have you painted it?' Una asked.

'No. I've recognised that it is beyond me. It is Greece—the whole of her history and her culture embodied in those echoing stones, and I haven't the arrogance to claim I could express that on canvas,' he replied.

It had been the first time she had heard him admit to inadequacy, and she loved him for it, for a recognition of his shortcomings which seemed to make him human as never before. By ever so slight a degree they had drawn more level with the evening's experience. They had walked as friends and had talked as friends, and before they parted, hope was on the wing.

But he *had* parted from her in the foyer—solicitous, attentive, escorting her to the lift and seeing her into it. And though for hour after hour she waited, her nerves elastic, her ears analysing every smallest sound, he did not come to join her. Nothing between them had changed.

CHAPTER SEVEN

THAT was the pattern of the rest of the nights they spent in Athens.

During the day Una would shop or visit the Museum and spend time with Daniel; Zante made professional calls and they both visited Daniel in the evening. They dined together at the hotel or a restaurant, and once went to the opera. But when Una retired to their room Zante let her go without a word as to his own intentions, and she set a stony resolve against asking where he spent his time until in the small hours—being asleep, she did not always know when—he came to bed and slept beside her or had already risen when she woke in the morning.

More than once she pretended to be asleep when she was not. But he never questioned her subterfuge if he were aware of it. When he joined her at as far distance as the wide bed would allow, she lay very still, determining he should not guess at her riot of longing to be touched in mastery and to touch in surrender.

By day they were all they pretended to be. By night they were as studiedly apart as two children who had quarrelled and were 'not speaking'. As a refinement of punishment Zante could hardly have devised a better, and the thought of the bizzare

situation's continuing when they took Daniel home
was a torture.

But when that happened, though Zante made
enough show of their cohabitation to deceive
Daniel's interest, by coming to her room night and
morning and making use of it during the day, he
did not share her bed again.

Daniel, a little more frail, but again on the right
side of danger, needless to say had eagerly and gratefully elected to stay on the island. He welcomed
Zante as his deputy organiser on the site and he had
experience of Una's expertise. The disbanded volunteers were coaxed back into service, and at first
from his bed, then from his sun-lounger in the garden and finally being driven to the site by Zante, he
again took a hand in his beloved project.

Zante was working all the hours there were. Besides going to the site every day, he was painting
for his Athens show.

It was to be on a Sunday, and he went over in
his own launch to catch the Saturday plane from
Corfu. Telling herself she could not endure the
farce of another night spent at the Theseus Palace,
Una dreaded his asking her to go with him—and
then was perversely irked that he did not. She had
mentally rehearsed making the excuse that she
could not leave Daniel in case he might need her,
and she was surprised and even piqued when for
once Zante did not try to demolish her will in favour
of his, but appeared to assume he would be going
alone.

On Sunday Madame Trepano came over to

luncheon with Maria. The conversation at table, though consisti g mainly of gossip and enquiries by each of them about the other's doings, was conducted in Eng ish for the benefit of Daniel and Una, and it was Daniel who, ignorant of the unwritten ban upon mention of Selene, innocently asked their guest, 'Your attractive daughter isn't with you today, Madame Trepano?'

Instantly Maria stiffened, as did Una with apprehension, as Madame Trepano replied, 'No. So kind of you to enquire. But yesterday she went over to Athens for what we learn from you to call "the weekend",' and Daniel waded deeper into danger by chiding gently,

'She is so young, Madame. You will allow her to go to Athens alone?'

At that an ejaculation by Maria was something between a sniff and a snort. But Madame Trepano rejected the suggestion with a slightly shocked, 'Alone? Indeed, no. Naturally she goes to welltrusted friends, where I know she will be safe,' and then tactfully dismissed the threat of Selene by smiling at Una and asking, 'Zante too is in Athens today, Maria tells me? And you not with him, my dear? That is bad, too bad. But it makes his return all the sweeter, hm?'

'Yes, of course.' Una had managed a thin smile in answer to the kindness. But inwardly she was seething. So! Selene on a weekend with "trusted friends"—how little parents sometimes knew! And Zante on professional business in Athens at the same weekend! It could—it just *could* be a coincidence, if Zante had suggested, however casually, that she, Una, should go with him. But obviously he had neither wanted nor meant her to go. For 'coincidence' read 'assignation', and he couldn't have guessed how Daniel's chance question would allow her to find out. He had cynically promised her that when he began or continued an affair with another woman, he would be discreet, and he thought he had been. But oh, Zante, *why*?

After luncheon the two ladies went to Maria's suite, Daniel repaired to the garden for his daily rest and Una walked down to the village to do some minor shopping. It was intensely hot and when she failed to get what she wanted in the little general store, she wandered out on to the quay to get some sea air.

The usual crowd of idlers knew her and nodded to her. She smilingly refused a drink from the man who serviced Zante's launch, and strolled on to his mooring bay where, as he had the launch, only the outboard motor dinghy was tied up. As she looked down at it from the jetty, she could not have said she had gone there with the intention of taking it out, but as she stood irresolute some private daemon tempted her to do *something* in defiance of Zante, in return for what her rioting imagination told her he would be doing with Selene for company in Athens.

She had never gone out in the dinghy. She had never been to Kassikona. Zante had said, 'When anyone has the sulks or just wants to be alone'. Well, she had good reason for sulking, hadn't she?

And she did badly need to be alone ... With the thought she was down the jetty steps and stepping into the boat. She untied her; the motor responded at once. She backed out, waved to the people on the quay and faced south for the tiny island. Someone shouted something to her, but it would have been in Greek and she wouldn't have understood. So she headed on towards her small adventure into mutiny and freedom.

Kassikona was not much more than an undulating rock covered in burnt grass. But Zante had mentioned a beach, so it must be possible to land. And it was. But in the tiny cove there was nothing to tie up to, so Una anchored the mooring rope under some flat stones before she climbed the sheltering rock to take a view of the rest of the terrain.

Zante had said too that there were some olives and some cabins, and somehow she had gained the impression that the primitive plaster houses huddled in the miniature valley she was overlooking were occupied by peasants who, probably, harvested the olives and tended a few sheep. But there was no sign of life except that of the swooping birds, and when she went down to explore the cabins they were all open but empty, their floors strewn with plaster detritus, their windows—one to each house—heat-warped, and their doors loose on their hinges.

There had been life there once, but there was none now. In spite of the overpowering heat Una shivered. No one had warned her that Erikona's 'baby' was as forlornly deserted as this. But she might as well press on and explore it all. Beyond the next range of rock there would be another valley and perhaps another beach to the sea, even a path by which she could make her way back to her original piece of shore and the boat.

The climb up and over the next ridge, owing to beetling overhangs which had to be bypassed circuitously, took longer than she thought. And when, tired and somewhat disenchanted with her escapade, she reached the summit, there was no valley beyond; no beach, no path, just unclimbable rock-face dropping sheer to an angrily lashing sea.

And that was strange. All that sucking and churning must be caused by jagged underwater rocks and inlets, for the sea from which she had beached on the other side of the island had been like the proverbial millpond. And there was no wind ...

Or was there? As she turned to retrace her steps, the only choice she had, she realised that there was wind now, and it was beating at her, streaming back her hair and bringing powdery dust with it to irritate her eyes. It was increasing, minute by minute, and the sun had gone in, without any lessening of the heat at all. Once she reached the valley she would have some protection. But then there was the lesser ridge before she came to the shore. She stood still to gauge the direction of the wind. It was from the north, the savage hot wind which plagued the near East, in North Africa under one name, in Arabia under another. Here it was the *meltemi*, and to touch even the nearest point of Erikona, which was Teriki Bay, she would have to steer due north into its ferocity, and she doubted her ability to do that.

Here it was coming at her from the side, some-times too strongly to fight against being bent and blown sideways like a sapling in a storm. She had passed the cabins now; next the ridge and then the welcome shore. But on the top of the ridge she halted, her parched lips agape with dismay. The shore—yes. But the surf which had lapped it silkily earlier was a white boiling like over-brimming hot milk. And—the dinghy was gone!

Slowly now, nagging herself for a fool and worse, she went down to investigate. Slabs of flat stone, but no mooring rope and no dinghy. And she, who had been taught the utmost respect for the wiles of moored craft, had let it happen! The wind would have teased at the stones—she saw they had shifted —the rope would have snaked away and the boiling sea had done the rest. By now the boat had drifted —how far south? Or had capsized? Or had been driven ashore and broken up?

What now? She had told no one where she had been heading. Perhaps that man who had shouted to her had wanted to ask, and by not pulling in and telling him she had broken another amateur sailors' rule. Her sulks against Zante had a great deal to answer for, and the full consequences she could not see.

It was nobody's business to notice when or whether the dinghy returned. Zante was due back in the late evening, but if the *meltemi* forced him to leave the launch berthed in Corfu and he had to return by the steamer if one were running, he might not notice the dinghy's absence either. And there was her father to worry about her, and Maria too, not to mention the loss of the dinghy at her hands. She wasn't asking Why? of Zante now; she was asking it of her own crass folly which had marooned her in this plight. She shivered again, dreading the dark which would be upon her in an hour and which she would have to endure until she and the dinghy were reported missing and a search was made. Even if the wind abated, she could not get away, and until it did, the only possible shelter from its fury was one of those dreary cabins. Wearily she turned and trudged down to them again.

She settled on some filthy sacking on the floor of the nearest she came to; sat, hugging her knees and listening to the wind ripping between the houses, and continually brushing herself free of the powdering plaster which flaked down from the ceiling and the walls.

She could not tell when the sun set. The piling clouds brought down the evening dark too soon. Presently and incredibly she was drowsing, her lullaby the crash of loose shutters and the squealing creak of door-hinges, and for all her discomfort she must have slept, for it was pitch dark when she woke, realising how cold she now was, and why. Her sweat-soaked shirt was clinging clammily to her; under it she wore nothing but her bra, but she stripped it off to allow it and her skin to dry. It was still dangling from her hand by its sleeve when, having heard nothing still but the clamour of the wind, she saw the door was being pushed open, and though rescue was all she had been praying for, she froze in alarm.

The arc of an electric torch raked her hideout, came to rest upon her dazzlingly. The man behind the torch was Zante.

'Oh——' Instinctively she hugged herself defensively, shirt still dangling. He swung the beam away from her and came forward. It was his eyes which raked her now, noting the nudity above her slacks, glancing at the shirt. 'So!' he gritted between his teeth. 'You arrant little fool, you trouble-seeking idiot! What do you think you are about? And where is the dinghy? Come here!'

She moved the few paces between them and looked up.

'It—— I didn't moor it properly, and the wind must have swept it away.'

'And where were you, that you let it go?'

'I'd gone to explore the island——'

'In the teeth of *that*?' The jerk of his head indicated the outdoors.

'The wind? It hadn't got up then; there was dead calm when I set out.'

'Ignoring the warning that was shouted to you—that the *meltemi* was on its way?'

'A man shouted from the quay, yes, but I didn't hear what he said. It—it was a lovely afternoon, and I wanted to see Kassikona, and I had *told* you I could manage a dinghy.' Her teeth were chattering now from cold and shock and fear of his justified anger.

'Manage a dinghy! You couldn't manage a scallop-shell in a bath,' he scoffed, and reached for her shirt. 'And what's this? Undressing in aid of what?'

'I'd got so hot, fighting the wind, that I was wet through with sweat. But I fell asleep, I don't know how I managed it, and when I woke I was so cold that I was just taking it off to dry it when you——when you——' She broke off. 'How did you—— know about me? How did you know where to look for me? Wh-what time is it?'

'Nine-ish. When I tied up, I saw the dinghy wasn't alongside, and when I asked around I heard you had taken it out and hadn't yet brought it back. The fellows thought you knew what you were about and when you took no notice of their warning, they concluded you were just taking a jaunt round or outside the harbour and left you to it.'

'You had to guess where I might have gone. Did you go up to the house to tell Father and Maria?' Una still found it difficult to call *To Aspro Spiti* 'home'.

'No. I rang them, and took out the launch again.'

'*Could* you? The wind, I mean?'

'It was behind me, but I'm not risking heading into it until it begins to drop, which it usually does after about six hours. We can probably get away by midnight.' He felt her shirt. 'This is still damp.'

'I know,' she nodded.

'And that?'

She cringed as his hand cupped her breast beneath her brassiere. 'That—that's all right.'

Zante frowned with annoyance, 'All the same, you should get it off.' As she hesitated, 'For pity's sake, I'm your husband! You can cut the prudery,' he rasped. 'Take it off, and you can wear my pull-over.' Divesting himself of it and tossing it to her, he added, 'I managed to drop anchor a wadeable distance out, but I shall have to carry you to the launch. Are you ready now?'

His arm closely about her, he kept her on his lee side as they struggled down to the shore, where he hoisted her in a fireman's lift over one shoulder, told her to hold on to his shirt, and waded into the surf. From her undignified position, looking down his back, she wryly compared this night with last, when for all she knew, Selene might have lain in abandon in his arms, whereas tonight she herself had for him only the nuisance value of an unnecessary burden.

The deeper water swished above his thigh-length waders and reached his waist before he made the launch. He boosted her over the side without ceremony and climbed aboard himself, then picked her up again and set her down on the double bunk in the little cabin.

'Did you get any sleep while you were waiting?' he asked.

'Some, yes. Fighting the wind made me so tired.'

'Then try to get a bit more now.' He pressed her back against the cushions and pulled a tartan rug over her, before turning his back on her to kick free of his waders and slacks and to unbutton his wet shirt. He stepped into another pair of slacks which he had taken from a drawer and came to lie, bare-torsoed, outside the rug beside her.

'I could use some rest myself,' he said. 'Helena laid on something of a riotous party last night.' Propping himself up on his elbow, he looked down at Una, rigid but quiveringly aware of his nearness which was not for her. 'You are not trying, lying there on your back and staring at the ceiling,' he accused. 'Come, turn on to your side and *try*.'

Resisting the temptation to turn inward to him, she obeyed by turning away, if only to avoid a scrutiny which held only practical concern for her; no invitation, no promise at all. Using her arm, bent at the elbow, as a pillow, she asked over her shoulder, 'How *was* the show? Did it go off well?'

'Helena was happy about it, which was all that mattered. And I sold a few canvases, made some contacts.'

Grasping a flowerless nettle which she knew would sting, 'Did you and Selene fly back to Corfu together?' Una asked.

At his half-caught breath she wished she had been facing him, to read whatever guilt there might be in his eyes. But on the surface, his echo of 'Selene? Yes, we came back on the same plane,' held only mild interest in the question.

'And *went* on the same plane on Saturday?'

'By chance, yes. But how did you know she was in Athens this weekend?'

Una told him how she knew. 'Was she at the show?' she asked.

'She came to it, yes.'

'And to the party on Saturday night?'

'Yes, she was there. Through me she knows Helena and a good many of her friends.'

'And after the show?' Una was nagging and she knew it, but she could not stop.

'We met again at the airport.' Zante paused. Then, 'Tell me, as a matter of interest only, of course! if I had asked you to come with me to stay at the Theseus Palace again, would you have come?'

'No.'

'Then do you consider you have any right to an hour-by-hour diary of my movements when I went to Athens alone?'

He must have known there was no answer to that, and she attempted none. She had learned nothing by her probing, except that he and Selene had had opportunity enough to betray her, and that she had already guessed.

She could not sleep again, but presently Zante did, as she could tell by his breathing without turning to look at him. He was restless, as he had not been during those traumatic nights at the Theseus Palace when they had each lain at the far sides of the huge bed, as remote as if they were not sharing it. Here a turn on to his back and another again on to his side on the economical width of the bunk brought his full weight against her back. His body shaped itself to the curve of hers, his even breath stirred her hair and he flung a relaxed arm across her waist.

She moved very slightly. He sighed, his lips murmured a sleepy protest, the arm tautened momentarily and the fingers of that hand found the hollow between her waist and the surface of the bunk, and clung. For that brief moment he was holding her, groping her closer to him, and the ache to turn fully into his arms, inevitably waking him, was almost unbearable. But the thought of his rejection of her when he woke deterred her. His physical reflexes in sleep had sought contact with the woman beside him. But his waking self wouldn't want to know her, wouldn't want to remember ...

She lay still until he shifted again and turned away. Even then she waited for some time before she slid stealthily off her side of the bunk, stood up, smoothed down his rumpled pullover over her hips, and stepped out of the cabin on to the deck.

The wind had dropped and the stars were out. Half an hour later she heard Zante stirring, and he came out on deck without asking how long she had been there.

He looked about him, gauging the weather conditions like an animal taking scent. He nodded. 'All right. Let's go,' he said, and took the wheel.

Even Daniel was censorious of Una's escapade with the dinghy, which the *meltemi* had beached just round the next headland from where it had drifted loose. Only Maria, strangely, voiced no blame in the affair, perhaps taking her side, Una suspected, because she was displeased with Zante. Primed by Madame Trepano's information, she claimed to Una that he must have known Selene was to be in Athens that weekend of his show, and how *could* he, she demanded, bristling, leave Una behind to lay himself open to the advances of that trollop who tried to make every man in sight her prey?

But whatever her reasons, Maria began to show a warm interest towards Una, and Una, remembering her early, desperate hope that she might find an ally in the older woman if only she could touch some chord in her, was grateful. At first, guarded, edging fearfully round any subject which might provoke Maria to one of her obsessive outbursts, she gradually drew her out to talk about herself, about her two husbands, even occasionally about Jason as a child. Maria could be amusing without bitterness about her schooldays in England, and when in the mood, she had a turn for mimicry of the social scene in Greece and Cyprus which she exploited to the full.

And then, one day, she was remembering Jason as a young man, speaking of him aloud in snatches, and Una tensed herself for the explosion which she felt was bound to follow.

'Handsome . . . as a young god. But you knew him, you say?' Una nodded Yes. 'Not a student, no. A lover of life, rather—of sport and fast cars; all things of the outdoors. And no doubt a breaker of hearts until——' Maria broke off. 'You found him so—a charmer?'

'I'm afraid I hardly knew him,' Una had to admit.

'And in England, *driven* there in his despair over that harpy, he would have lost his sparkle, his zest. He joins a university, but he does not like to study. He is unhappy. He drifts. But when I beg him, he will not come home. *She* is still here and has hopes of Zante. So he stays in England and *mourns*,' Maria concluded dramatically.

'And yet, you know, when Zante went over to England after the—accident, he found that by then Jason had another girl, so he must, partly at least, have got over Selene,' Una reminded her.

'He was a young man with a young man's needs, so he may have tried to console himself with some-one else,' Maria allowed.

'Though you wouldn't have had him marry Selene if she didn't love him?'

Maria pursed her lips. 'In Greece we see it as a woman's pleasure and duty to love her husband,' she ruled. 'And if Jason had not taken offence at her No to him—because at that time she saw Zante as the greater prize—and he had stayed here to wear her down, she might have been glad to take him in the end, and *I* should still have had a son at my side, and perhaps grandchildren at my knee, instead of —of a suicide in the shameful grave to which his enemies drove him!'

Because her tone was sad, rather than vitupera-tive, Una took courage to argue, 'Dear Maria, you only torture yourself by thinking so——'

'I am not the only one. Zante believes it too.'

(As I know to my cost, thought Una.) Aloud she said, 'But neither of you can know it for certain,

against all the evidence to the contrary. Think——'
she urged. 'Jason was young, with everything before
him. He had been in our country long enough to
know that first offenders—which was all he was—
are dealt with very leniently. At most, he would have
earned a suspended sentence, and he would *not*
have committed suicide for fear of that. Please,
Maria, do try to believe I could be right!'

As, for once, Maria made no stubbornly convinced reply, and as a thought struck her, Una dared
further. 'I realise that perhaps I shouldn't say this,'
she began slowly. 'But I wonder—are you quite,
quite sure that because you have a grudge against
Selene Trepano, you have not *wanted* to believe
that Jason killed himself, in order to blame her for
his having gone to England at all?'

It was twisted reasoning, Una knew, but it was
just possible, and if Maria were honest she might
admit it. Una held her breath, waiting. Maria stared
at her beringed hands in silence.

Then: 'You think I *want* my only son dead—out
of revenge?'

Una's compassion welled. 'Dear,' she said, 'you
have had to accept that he's dead, but it wasn't by
his own hand, nor anyone's fault, least of all Selene's.
It was an accident, as everyone connected with him
knew at the time—the Museum, the coroner, myself,
and as only you and Zante refused to believe it, I
thought—well, that there had to be a reason for
your standing out, and that your resentment against
Selene might be it.'

Another silence until Maria said, 'You are very—

shrewd. You are young, but you know already that revenge is a very strong emotion. How is that?'

Una could have told her, but did not. 'I only know that when it's strong enough, it's blind to all persuasion against,' she said.

'When one has been mortally wounded, it is one's way of meting out justice,' Maria parried. 'But perhaps you are a little right—I may have hated so much that only to lay the blackest of guilt on the right shoulders has satisfied me. You think I may have been not only mistaken about Jason's death, but vindictive too? Is that so?'

Una nodded. 'But with cause,' she said.

'And Zante? He has been as persuaded as I that Jason was cruelly wronged. So whom would you say *he* has hated enough to believe that person responsible for Jason's death?'

'I—don't know. He may have had different reasons from yours.'

'But you do not know? Then you have not talked with him about this as you have with me?'

'No.'

'Why not?'

'I—suppose I haven't thought he would listen.'

'*I* have listened,' Maria pointed out with reason. 'Or is it that you think it unwifelike to put your husband in the wrong?'

For want of a better reply, Una murmured, 'Perhaps.'

'Ah. And very proper too,' Maria nodded sagely. 'Though when you have a little more experience of marriage, my dear, you will learn that there are times—in an intimate moment, or after an hour of shared love—when a wife may persuade her husband to any of her views and he will listen. You will remember that?'

Una forced a wan smile. 'I'll try,' she said.

CHAPTER EIGHT

So, with Maria reluctantly half-persuaded of Jason's accidental death, what hope was there of her as an ally against Zante's cruel conviction otherwise?

Very little, it seemed. She must have told Zante she had been moved by Una's reasoned argument, but the effect upon his own prejudice was nil, as Una was to find out when he remarked one morning,

'I hear you have been using the soft answer on Maria—with some success?'

Una pretended not to understand. 'What soft answer?' she queried.

'The one that turneth away wrath, of course. Very subtle of you. But if you think you can alter the facts about Jason, I'm afraid you are sadly mistaken. In my view they point only one way.'

'Even though everyone else involved, including the police and the coroner, believed they pointed exactly the other?' Suddenly enraged for Maria's sake, as much as for her own, Una exploded, 'Of course, even in the teeth of absolute proof, you'll maintain that I was responsible——'

'Though not in Maria's hearing. Credit me with some discretion, please!'

'And that, not to protect me, but to keep the peace in your household,' she flashed. His interjection had broken the thread of her argument, but she picked it up. 'As I was saying, you will believe what you will, because the Diomed family pride could never admit to being wrong, could it? But why you should want to persuade Maria that her son committed suicide is completely beyond me!' she declared hotly.

'I didn't have to persuade her. The conviction came as naturally to her as to me.'

'I don't believe it. She wasn't in England. She didn't hear the evidence. She must have been influenced by what you came back and told her.'

'No. She was Jason's mother, and she knew him, as I did, for the mercurial character he was. Up today, down tomorrow, and to be accused when he was innocent——'

'But he wasn't innocent! He *had* stolen the vase and the other things!'

'Very well—accused and arraigned,' Zante conceded evenly. 'That would be enough to send his spirit plummeting to the depth where, for honour's sake, suicide would have appeared to him as the only answer. It was the only gesture he could make to his mother. He made it. At the time she recognised it for what it was, and for all your well-meant ministrations, my dear, I suspect that in her heart she still does.'

'As you do too,' Una said despairingly.

'As I do too,' he confirmed.

'So that, even in the face of irrefutable evidence otherwise, you wouldn't let Maria accept it, nor accept it yourself,' Una stated, rather than asked.

Zante shrugged. 'You carry the argument to the

absurd. If it were really "irrefutable", I should have to accept it, shouldn't I?'

Una shook her head. 'Maria might. In fact, I think she would now be glad to. But *you* wouldn't.'

'You think not? Why?'

'Because it would rob you of your revenge on me. And that you need. It's as valuable to you as your family pride and honour, isn't it, Zante Diomed?' For a long moment her eyes challenged the blue inscrutability of his before she turned and left him, convinced that he could not deny the accusation.

Without much reward to date the work on the dig went on. For days of patient search nothing of importance to Daniel's records would be found, and though every shard of earthenware or corroded piece of metal would be washed, bagged and entered up, they had all proved to be of Greek origin, without any of the Egyptian influence for which he was looking.

As the summer heat intensified the island was apt to suffer a caprice of weather which brought down upon it an enveloping fog which was as sudden and as local as Daniel reminded Una had been the fitful river-mists which would swirl up from the low-lying Falcon river at home, as baffling and blinding until they dispersed as were the heat-fogs over Erikona. Then, when everything dripped moisture and the dry, easily worked soil became temporarily slabs of solid pudding, the enthusiasm of the amateur excavators was apt to

wane, and the competition for washing and bagging
rather than for digging was considerable.

So that, on a morning of such conditions, only a
few stalwarts, among them Roland and Una, were
working on their plots, when Roland, dispiritedly
spooning and scraping a few minutes earlier, suddenly alerted Una with an excited, 'Something
here! Metal ... and curved ... And I do believe—
whole!'

Oblivious of the caked mud Una felt her way
over to him and helped to scrabble while he addressed the object, 'Come out, you pesky so-and-so,'
and then ordered her, 'Bring over that pick. It's
too deep for trowels.'

As he worked and levered with the pick, she
warned, 'Don't dent it, for pity's sake. If it *is* whole,
it could be a vase——' and then had to laugh ruefully with him when their find heaved up to his
leverage—metal indeed and certainly in one piece,
but blackened and battered out of all the symmetry
which might once have made it a vase.

Roland wiped sweat out of his eyes and daubed
it down his grimy cheek. ' "Don't *dent* it!" the
woman said! Looks like someone took a sledge-
hammer to it a few aeons ago,' he gurgled.

Una defended it. 'Don't be beastly to it. Its neck
is quite graceful and they can hammer the rest
out.' She scrubbed at the metal. 'Bronze, I believe.
And do you realise it's the very first *whole* thing
we've turned up? Let's take it to the office and
report.'

It was dampening that neither Daniel nor Zante

had yet arrived, having gone first to collect the
mail from the harbour post office. But when Una
ran to help Daniel out of her car and to tell their
news, he was gratifyingly impressed, and thrusting
the bundle of letters into her hand, he almost
scuttled into her office ahead of her.

He handled the vase as if it were porcelain. 'Yes,
bronze,' he confirmed. 'About sixth century B.C.
You noticed this?' stroking the almost undamaged
handle from the shoulder to the vase's lip. 'Open-
work in the form of a lotus? And this'—tracing
beneath the dirt of the curved neck—'raised work,
letters beaten in, a name?'

Neither Una nor Roland had noticed either and
said so.

'Yes, well,' said Daniel, bright eyes twinkling,
'as it happens, both are characteristic of an authenti-
cated sixth-century bronze vase found on the mainland and now in the Corinth Museum. Same lattice
scroll work of the handle—typically Egyptian, that.
And a name, the name of a king, an Egyptian king
named Bocchoris, I haven't much doubt, though
I can't read it here for dirt, on its collar!'

He waited, obviously savouring the effect upon
his audience. Most people were content to gasp, and
it was Zante who questioned,

'So you are entitled to hope the Egyptians did
come here to trade?'

'On a single find, that would be too much,' Daniel
admitted. 'But if here, then they'll have gone to the
other small out-islands too, and that's what I want
to prove.'

'Then isn't this the time for you to shout Eureka?' asked Zante.

'*I am* shouting it for all I'm worth—inside,' replied Daniel happily.

Everyone now was willing to troop back on the search which was to be rewarded at intervals by the finding of a few scarabs and seals, though nothing as characteristically Egyptian as the vase. But Daniel, his faith and his work justified, was content. The rest would follow ...

Zante went back to the house for wine in which the find was toasted from picnic beakers; Roland, by luck rather than by merit, was the hero of the hour, and the whole site was en fête until sundown. By then the mist had cleared, disappearing within minutes over the sea like a rolled-up blanket, and when the White House party returned Una lingered in the garden before going to bath and change for dinner. She stretched out on Daniel's sun-lounger, only then realising, from the crackle in the pocket of her shirt, that she was still carrying the packet of letters he had handed her.

She took them out and looked them through. Nothing for her from England, three for Daniel, one she recognised as from Zante's English agent, and another for him, a private handwritten envelope with a Falconbridge postmark just discernible.

She eyed it curiously. She didn't know he corresponded with anyone in Falconbridge, unless with his hostess there, 'Mrs Vice-Chancellor', and somehow the stationery hadn't that lady's class.

She put speculation about it from her mind,

turning to wonder what her father's confident mental shout of 'I have found!' was going to mean to her own future.

If other finds followed the first, he was established here until the end of the summer. If other finds followed today's, he would not abandon the site. He would come back, and probably to other of the smaller islands, in the spring. And she would be faced with a never-ending prospect of keeping the truth of her marriage from him. No escape for her to England with him or on his account. While Zante's vendetta continued she had to live this lie for Daniel's sake. How was she going to bear it?

Owing to Daniel's happy mood, dinner was almost a convivial affair, with even Maria relaxed enough to emerge from her shell of reserve and to laugh with him. After dinner they listened to a programme of haunting Greek music on the stereo, and they broke up late to go to their rooms.

Una did not close her shutters on to the still night, and when she woke the sky was streaked with a lighter grey, promising dawn, though it was still dark. There were sounds of movement from Zante's room. She sat up, listening intently, half dreading, half hoping that he might be coming through to her in a friendly aftermath to the successful day and evening.

She heard his studio door open and presently he was back in his room, still moving about. Then his door to the corridor opened stealthily, and upon a sudden reckless impulse, barefoot and without a robe, she was at her own door, meeting him.

He was dressed, in shirt and slacks and his knapsack of painting gear was slung over one shoulder. He looked her over. 'It's not time to get up. Go back to bed,' he ordered.

She did not move. 'Wh-where are you going?' she asked.

'Painting. I want to catch the pre-dawn light on Archon.'

'I was awake and I heard you moving. Could I come with you?' Playing it lightly and greatly daring, she added, 'Don't you remember I once threatened that if you went painting at night, I should expect to be invited to go along?'

He nodded. 'Different days, those. And I prefer to work alone.'

Irked by the snub, her daemon of malice rose. 'Even though you may need an anonymous model, as you did for *The Sea, The Sea!* and used Selene?' she taunted.

'I don't need a model for dawn over Archon. It will stand by its own quality, I hope.'

'I see,' she said, her temper deflated.

'Good.' He took a step or two away from her, then turned. 'Go and get dressed, if you like,' he said. 'I'll wait for you in the car.'

Archon was a lonely stretch of shore on the east of the island, running down to a phosphorescent sea which sparked with blue and green light by day but which lay grey and quiet under the dawn clouds of morning. The scene was a study in shades of grey, of the white of sand and the black brush-shaped strokes of the pointed cypresses which

sprang from the stark red rocks climbing up and
back from the shore.

The air was already warm and scarcely stirring.
Zante set up his easel and canvas on which he had
sketched his subject in rough. Una sat near by on
the sand, aware of and grateful for something of
the same rapport she had shared with him on the
day he had taken her swimming. That, she had
suspected at the time, had been to impress her
father with their honeymoon intimacy. But this
morning there had been no one there to impress,
so what new tolerance of her might have allowed
her to come? At least she would hope he felt some.
Or was it abject of her to hope?

He painted for a time, ignoring her. Then he sat
back, frowning. 'No,' he said. 'No, I was wrong.
There's not enough colour, no point of value to
catch the eye.' And then he suddenly shot at her,
'How would you fancy yourself as a sea-nymph,
surfacing at dawn?'

'A—sea-nymph?' she echoed, not undersanding.

'I don't mean a buxom Aphrodite rising from
the waves, all panache and self-confidence, but a
shy girl, discovering the shallows and land for
perhaps the first time. Well?'

'In—in your picture, you mean?' She shook her
head. 'No, you couldn't want—— And I couldn't
——'

His stare of appraisal embarrassed her. 'Well, obviously not, in jeans and shirt,' he agreed, leaving
his meaning clear.

'I—haven't anything else,' she said, avoiding his eyes.

'You don't need anything else.' He laid aside his brush and came over to her. 'Come, will you try a pose?'

She stood up 'You mean—in the nude?' she asked, knowing he did. 'I couldn't. I wouldn't know how.'

'It's for me to tell you how, and whether I can use you,' he corrected. 'But if you can't tell the difference between an academic exercise and an improper suggestion, forget it.'

That stung her. She looked about her. Empty sky, empty sea, empty shore. No curious, prurient eyes on the watch. Just herself and Zante, his awareness of her only 'academic', her body one that he had no desire to know. The chill of the thought was almost physical, but it was a challenge. 'Very well,' she murmured, and turning her back on him, she slowly unbuttoned her shirt.

He was waiting for her on the edge of the surf. He told her to wade in nearly knee-deep, then to turn about. 'You are coming out of the sea, not stepping in for a paddle,' he explained, and stood back, viewing her beneath narrowed lids when she obeyed.

'No,' he said irritably of her nervously concealing hands. 'You are a child of nature with no inhibitions. You are as unconscious of nakedness as was Eve. You are used to deep water, but sand and light and foam are new wonders to you, wholly strange. So play with them, kick fountains——' After a minute or two, 'Yes, like that,' he said, and went back to his canvas.

Having accepted his challenge, Una tried to act her part by thinking herself back into a childhood when her first experience of a seashore had indeed been a magic never to be known in quite the same way again. This was seaside, she was pretending, all its pleasures for her, when suddenly a great slash of Zante's brush must have obliterated most of his work.

She looked across at him, startled. 'No,' he said again, then went for her clothes and brought them down to her.

She approached him and took them from him. At less than an arm's distance between them they faced each other in tableau immobility. Though he was dressed she could visualise beneath the thin stuff of his shirt, the powerful shoulders, the hard male torso which should be hers to caress. He was her husband, wasn't he? Did he think for a moment she would have undressed for him if he weren't? So how dared he study her body—so *clinically*? And —dear God—touch it too!

For his hand had gone out to her. A fingertip traced a line from temple to jaw, followed the long curve of her neck, moved aside to touch the hollow of her throat, and back again to the smooth fall of her shoulder, then to circle the swell of breast, and so over her rib cage to her waist.

Desire for him sprang into flame and burned. Surely? Now? But the finger's titillating passage had stopped. It had only been the detached exploration of an artist after all, and when he turned away she knew she shouldn't have hoped.

When she joined him, waiting for him to pack his gear, 'What was the matter?' she asked. 'Was it a mistake, asking me to pose for you?'

He nodded. 'A bad one,' he said tautly.

That was unfair. 'I'm sorry, but I've never done anything of the sort before. How could I know what you wanted of me?' she defended herself.

He looked down at her briefly. 'No, how could you?' he echoed with a finality which invited no argument.

On the drive back he told her, 'I am going to England tomorrow.'

'To England? For how long?'

He shrugged. 'As long as my business takes me.'

She remembered the letter from his agent which she had left for him in the hall last night before going to change. 'To put on a show?' she asked, working out the connection.

'Not this time. On other business. While I am away, Giorgio can drive you and Daniel to the dig.'

If she had been a real wife, sharing his interests, he wouldn't have dared to be so reticent. Irked, she retorted, 'I'm surprised you aren't afraid I might run away while you are gone!'

He shook his head. 'I don't have to be afraid. You aren't chained to a wall. You could "run" any time you could get to the airport. It's your conscience that keeps you here.'

'I *have* no bad conscience about Jason Mithredes!' she denied indignantly.

'But you have one towards your father and Maria which I think will keep you here,' he replied shrewdly.

'Only because you suggested I must have.'

'And a good enough reason, surely? And as you saw the wisdom of obeying, yes, I think you will still be here when I come back,' he said unanswerably except with a vituperation which Una knew he could match and outdo if she attempted it. She said nothing, and only later remembered he had had another letter from England by the day's post. Had that any connection with his errand? she wondered. But snubbed enough already, she would not ask.

Zante left the next day, piloting his own launch to Corfu, undertaking some professional messages for Daniel and leaving the address of his London club with Una.

She and Daniel went to the site as usual and two days later were rewarded with the finding of an authentic Egyptian bronze mirror and some tableware carved with figures in the unmistakably formal poses of Egyptian friezes.

Daniel was delighted, his theories about the two-way traffic between Egypt and the Greek islands proved.

'Mercenary soldiers and ships and wine from the Greeks to the Egyptians, and from them, domestic platters and glass and trinkets for their women,' he triumphed, entirely innocent of the part his success played in Una's bleak future.

Sometimes she rehearsed admitting to him that her marriage was no marriage. But, as Zante had shown he knew only too well, it was a rehearsal for something which would not happen. She could not buy her freedom at Daniel's expense. Besides— something which Zante did not know—though her dignity might want freedom from him, her love did not.

Zante had been away for a week and she had not seen Roland Luard, now nearing the end of his sabbatical, since the day of his original find on the site. Selene too, as well as her loss of interest in the dig, seemed to have an uncanny knack (or prior knowledge?) of learning when Zante would be absent from it, and as far as Una knew, she had not been over to the island since before he had gone to England. Once Una woke from a jealousy- prompted nightmare to the suspicion that they might be together. But the next she was to hear of Selene came from Madame Trepano, distressed and anxious, on a visit to Maria.

They were together in the salon when Una came in from the site. Selene's mother was twisting a damp handkerchief into a rag, and Maria's dour comfort for her friend was marred by her dark censure of Selene.

'Selene Trepano, the ingrate, has left home— gone—run away,' she explained to Una. 'And that with no more of a message to her mother than that she has "gone to friends" and that she will be "in

touch later". Dorcas here wants to believe her, but
man-mad as she is, it is my belief she has gone to
one of them—and to her ruin.'

Una's heart missed a beat. Selene had 'gone to
friends' in Athens when she had contrived to be
there at the same time as Zante. Was history re-
peating itself? Could Selene have followed him
to England? But at Madame Trepano's little moan
of protest over 'man-mad', Una turned to her. 'I'm
so sorry, Madame. She didn't let you guess where
she might be?'

A sad shake of Madame's head. 'No word of that.
We have friends in Athens, in Italy, in Cyprus,
but they hear nothing of her. I have telephoned——'

'Just a moment, Madame——' Una had remembered something. 'Italy?' she questioned. 'Isn't your
cousin, Signor Varani, Italian? Have you been in
touch with him?'

'Florio Varani? No. I do not know where he is. He
travels widely. He is very—public. And he scorns
Selene as a silly little girl. He hurts her gentle feel-
ings. She would not go to him.'

Una was not so sure. If Selene were not with
Zante, she might well be in pursuit of her other
ambitions—to be made a star. 'Even though, as you
must know, she hoped he could help her to a career
in films or in modelling?' Una prompted.

'No, no! This I cannot believe—that she would
sink to begging his patronage. Of course I know
about her foolish hopes, but he would do nothing
for her. I would not *permit* him to help her.'

Madame's chin trembled. 'He is not, you understand, the kind of man to whom I could entrust
her. He is worldly, a libertine—no sort for a young
girl as innocent as Selene.'

'Huh! *Innocent?*' snorted Maria, and Una advised,

'All the same, oughtn't you try to find him?
If only, supposing Selene is with him, to persuade
her to come home?'

It was a suggestion which had the approval of
Maria, who agreed, 'Yes, Dorcas, that is what you
should do. You must have addresses of the places
he frequents—film studios, theatres, clubs—and he
can be traced.'

'He could be abroad—London, America—anywhere!' her friend wailed.

'Then all the more reason for doing nothing tonight,' Maria resolved for her. 'Myself, I would
leave the girl to her wanton ways. Disappointed of
Zante when he married Una, she now flaunts herself elsewhere to attract his notice, regardless of the
pain for you. You should not fret for her, Dorcas.
But one must suppose that a daughter is a daughter,
as a son is a son——' Maria's teeth closed briefly on
her lips as she paused before adding, 'And so you
will stay with us tonight. No excuses.'

Madame Trepano protested faintly, 'You are not
always—kind, Maria. Selene is a *good* girl.' She
looked at her watch. 'The steamer——'

'Will leave without you,' Maria decided. 'Come
now, I shall see you to bed myself, and bring you
a hot cognac and milk.'

Una had never seen Maria so resolute, so aggressively in command. It was as if Zante's mantle of authority had descended on her shoulders. Or was it that in her friend's trouble, she was able to forget her own? It could happen, Una knew, and she wondered whether, happening to Maria, it could make a new person of her, looking forward, instead of despairingly back.

Except on the site, where everything continued to promise well, the next several days were negative in more directions than one. Zante neither wrote nor telephoned, Florio Varani was not traced, and her mother had no news of Selene. Once Maria confided to Una that she and Dorcas Trepano had sometimes discussed their setting up a home together.

'But always, always, it is that girl who is the thorn in the flesh,'—meaning Maria's flesh, Una assumed —'and so it has come to nothing. For to tolerate a friend's little faults day by day is one thing, but to live alongside a heartless strumpet like Selene Trepano would be quite another,' Maria concluded self-righteously.

It was on one of these frustrating days that Una gave in to Daniel's suggestion that she should take a few days' holiday on her own on the mainland, say in Athens or Delphi or Corinth.

Una was tempted, but, 'You wouldn't mind my going?' she questioned anxiously.

'Of course not, love,' he assured her.

'But Zante might telephone or suddenly arrive back,' she demurred.

'If he does, you will have let us know where you will be, and we can tell him, or we can send him to join you. It always does a young husband good to realise his wife has an existence apart from him,' Daniel stated sagely. 'For instance, I remember——'

Una laughed again at his oft-told tale of how her mother, a passionate animal lover, had cut short her honeymoon by a day in order to attend a 'Help Our Pets' conference—and decided to go again to Athens.

She went over to Corfu for the next morning's flight, and not knowing of any hotel but the Theseus Palace, she booked in there again, hoping she might exorcise the unhappy memories it had for her, by enjoying a spell in a quiet single room without associations.

She dined in the hotel that evening and afterwards went early to bed, shutting out the thought of the Parthenon, which, without Zante, she felt she could not bear to visit again for a very long time.

The next morning she window-shopped and made a few purchases, lunched at a pavement café to haunting zither music, and when the Museum reopened after the siesta hour, she went there again. Tomorrow she would——

But her plans for the next day were never to take shape. At the hotel reception desk when she asked for her key, the clerk turned to the key-bank and turned again with an apologetic smile.

'I am sorry, Madame Diomed, but Kyrios Diomed is out and seems to have it with him.'

Una stared, open-mouthed. On this, only her

second visit, she had been instantly recognised by the staff, so she had only asked for 'my key' without quoting the number of her single room. But 'Kyrios Diomed'? They must suppose she was here with Zante, who wasn't ... couldn't be. *Or could he?* Suppose he hadn't gone to England at all, but he had been in Athens all the time on some secret purpose of his own? She felt physically sick at the thought of how easily he could lie to her and be believed, and wondered if she had made her dismay visible when the clerk said helpfully, 'There is no problem. If Madame cares to mount, the floor-maid will show her into the apartment with her pass-key.' He picked up the house phone. 'I shall ring the floor and she will be waiting when Madame arrives.'

Una put out a detaining hand. 'No. No, it doesn't matter. Later perhaps, if my husband hasn't returned, but I'll take tea in the restaurant first.'

From where she stood she had been able to see her own key on its hook, but she would not ask for it. She would watch herself for Zante's return, and chose a hidden corner behind a giant palm to do so. If he came in by the main doors she could not miss him, and though he might use the entrance from the car-park instead, he must go to his suite some time, and she had all the evening and night for a vigil which was the only thing which could satisfy her vengeful need of a confrontation with Zante at a disadvantage he could not possibly foresee.

During the long hour and longer—nearly two—which she waited, eyes strained on the entrance to the foyer, occasionally she allowed him the benefit of the possibility that he might indeed be only staying over one night in Athens on his return. But his long silence, his effrontery in staying at the Theseus Palace if, as she suspected, he were enjoying some amorous interlude, hardened her resolve to continue her spying until he appeared, or until she had to conclude she had missed him, or that he wasn't going to return that night. Until——

Suddenly he was there. At the reception desk, joking with a different clerk from the one who had attended her. And though he was alone there, *he had not been alone when he came in.* The woman who had entered with him had already crossed to the elevators, out of Una's view. Her eyes, tired of their long focusing though they were, had not deceived her. Zante and the girl of whom she had had that brief glimpse were together. She would swear to it, and the girl would be waiting for him to join her at the elevators.

Selene—or who?

CHAPTER NINE

THE girl was a stranger.

Crossing the foyer from different directions, Una and Zante converged upon her simultaneously. Her puzzled look questioned Una's arrival, but Una was disappointed of any shocked or guilty surprise on Zante's part. As if he had expected to meet her there at just that moment, he introduced them smoothly and formally.

'Una—Mrs Coburn. Mrs Coburn—meet Una, my wife,' and added to Una a satiric, 'You anticipate my every command! How did you know I was going to call you to meet us here?'

'Us'!—linking himself and his Mrs Coburn together! Una told him shortly, 'I didn't. I came over to do some more sightseeing and some shopping.'

'When?'

'I booked in last night.'

'They should have told me.'

They had let one elevator depart without them, and while they waited for the next, Una asked his companion, 'Do you live in Athens, Mrs Coburn?'

'Do I——? Oh no!' The nervous flush which suffused the girl's pretty young face rejected the very idea. 'I'm from England. This is the first time

I've been to Greece. Just on a short visit—only a few days.'

Una dropped a glance at the ring on the girl's third finger. 'With your husband? Or—at the invitation of mine?' she queried cruelly, hating herself for using the girl as a weapon against Zante, but determined to pierce his debonair nonchalance if she could.

Her victim flushed hotly again. 'At—at——' she hesitated, lifting appealing eyes to Zante, who interposed briskly,

'At mine. Lorna's husband is with the Nato Forces in Europe and isn't due for leave just now.'

'I see.' The clipped words implied that Una saw nothing which she either understood or liked, and neither of the others had replied when the elevator stopped.

Una watched as Zante dropped one of the two room-keys he held into Lorna Coburn's hand. (So —the same floor, but separate rooms. At least Zante was discreet enough to observe the hotel's proprieties, she thought cynically.) Before they parted he invited the girl, 'Dinner—here at nine?' and at her nod, watched her down the corridor in one direction before, a hand under Una's elbow, he took the other.

She shook free of the hand but went with him, recognising the suite he opened up as the one they had shared before. He must have noticed the glance of recoil she gave it as he closed the door behind them, for he questioned, 'In the circumstances as you see them, I daresay you are thinking me guilty of the worst of taste, as well as of all the rest—lies, infidelity, seduction of a married woman, even of cradle-snatching—who knows?'

Una winced at the taunt. She said with difficulty, 'And *I* daresay I should have been prepared for the circumstances I've found. After all, you promised me that "if and when" you took another woman to your bed, you wouldn't shame me in front of my— your friends. So I suppose I should be grateful that you went as far as England to find her, and no nearer than Athens to enjoy her on a stolen week-end. Though, in view of the people who know you here, and this place apparently your home-from-home, I'd have thought that was too near for safety—wouldn't you? And as for cradle-snatching, well—I know you like them young. Selene——'

'You can leave Selene out of this,' Zante rasped.

'Willingly, since you're cheating on her as well as me,' Una allowed. 'Meanwhile, your latest conquest—who is she?'

He did not answer at once. Then, flatly, 'She is your "irrefutable evidence",' he said.

She stared at him. 'My——'

'Which you doubted I would accept, even if it hit me in the face,' he reminded her.

She recalled her taunt of him, never supposing it had touched him for longer than she had taken to fling it at him. Bewilderedly, 'I don't understand,' she told him. 'You mean—evidence of how Jason died? But—this woman? What can she know about it? Who *is* she?' she appealed again.

Zante crossed the room to face her. 'She was Jason's girl,' he said. 'The one you didn't know he had, but whom I traced and saw when I was in England after his death. Lorna Blyth then. She has married since.'

Una tried to work it out. 'You saw her and talked to her? But if she has proof now that he didn't commit suicide, why didn't she know then? Or if she did know then, why didn't she tell you? Why did she let you disagree with the verdict on him, and believe otherwise?'

'Because she believed it herself at the time. Like his mother and me, *she* thought he had taken his life for honour's sake.' Zante motioned Una to a chair. 'Sit down. It's a story I'd have preferred you should hear from her, and I planned that you should. But this is the gist——

'She loved Jason. She had left home to live with him, and was waiting for him when he came back from Egypt in disgrace. She worked herself, had saved, and she put up the bail for him. She thought she was pregnant by him, had told him so, and she believed that this and his pending trial had driven him to suicide——'

Una said, 'Wait. She told you this when you first traced her?'

'Not then. She was living again with her mother after his death, and she has only told me now she was afraid I should despise her if she had confessed the truth of his seduction of her then. Her fear of her pregnancy had been a false alarm, but she mourned Jason for the cruelly ill-used and faithful lover she thought him, until chance took a hand in proving to her he had been neither.'

Una moistened her dry lips. 'What chance?' she asked.

'Sentimentally she had kept some of his clothes, among them a favourite old jacket. With a kind of reverence she had folded them away until, when she had fallen in love again, she realised it was a feeling she couldn't expect her fiancé to share. So he prepared to get rid of them and found in the pocket of the jacket a letter to another woman which told the whole sordid story. It laid plans for his leaving Lorna the day after the night on which he was to die. No suicide envisaged—only a gloating over his ability to skip his bail and get out of the country with his new girl-friend who, as one might have guessed, would be funding the operation. He even had the gall to quote Lorna's pregnancy as just one side of a "dirty business" he would be escaping.' Zante paused, then added, 'She admits that if she had known him for what he was at the time, it would have broken her completely.'

Una drew a long breath of compassion. 'But she's happy now?'

'Blissfully, I gather. She married a month ago and wrote the truth about Jason to me as soon as her husband had gone back to his regiment.'

'You had a private letter from Falconbridge,' Una remembered aloud. 'How did she know where you were?'

'I had asked her to get in touch with me if she ever learned anything which bore upon what we both thought then was not much of a mystery about Jason's death.'

'And the news she gave you took you to England——'

'Yes. Though in fact, only that same day something had put the first doubt of his suicide into my mind. Do you remember a particular morning of heat-fog on the site?'

Wonderingly, 'Yes?'

'And how Daniel likened it to sudden swirls of localised river-fog from the Falcon? Well, that gave me to wonder whether Jason might have driven his car blindly into one of them, and so into the river. When I went to England again I checked with the weathermen and learned that there had been some fitful fogs around that time. But when you gave me Lorna's letter, I was still having to wonder, and knew I must find out.'

'Because—because if that was really what happened, it meant that—no one was to blame for his suicide, hounding him to his death? It meant that I——! Oh, Zante, why didn't you tell me? It would have saved me so much!' Una appealed.

'So much—what?'

She looked away. 'Jealousy. Doubt of you. They had told me at the desk that you were here, and when you came in with a woman, I thought—I was so humiliated and angry that you should dare to bring her here where you are known, and they know me, I almost gloated over finding you out, confronting you, putting you in the wrong *in front of her*. When all the while you'd been on

an errand to clear me——!' she finished brokenly,
willing him to accept a contrition she didn't know
how to put into words.

She felt his hand upon her shoulder. Then it
went to her chin, forcing her to look up into his
face.

'You could say, I suppose, that I'd asked for your
jealousy of me,' he conceded. 'In any case, beside
the enormity of my doubt of you, does it compare?'

'At least you were fair enough and just enough,
once you questioned whether you might be wrong,
to do something about it,' she muttered.

'Fair? Just?' he echoed savagely, and flung away
from her. With his back turned, 'Do you suppose
anything as calculated as either fairness or justice
sent me bolting to England?' he asked.

'What, then?'

'It was hope.'

Una warmed to the word. 'You hoped I shouldn't
be as guilty as you thought me? I'm—glad. Thank
you,' she said, meaning deep gratitude, and was
totally unprepared for the violence with which he
turned upon her and drew to her feet, pinioning
her so closely that she was as conscious of his heart-
beats as of her own.

'Thank you!' he mimicked her tone again. 'As if
I'd done you a minor charity! It means so little to
you, does it, that you can dismiss with a polite
"thank you" the love I've had to check—and check
again, over and over—while I thought you had to
be punished for your part in sending Jason to his
death? So,—polite child—"Thank you", you say,

while I—heart and body and mind—shout praise to all the powers there be for setting me free—free, do you hear?—to love you as I do?' He allowed himself a shrug of despair. 'But no, you haven't been through the awful frustration of it. It's asking too much that you should understand.'

Looking back over the bleak nights and days of his rejection of her, Una wondered if he had any idea of her own suffering at his hands. She whispered, 'If you had to punish me, you should have sent me away, not brought me here to refuse yourself to me. And if you *have* loved me, if only you could have weakened just once; denied your conscience and made love to me because you couldn't help it, *then* I'd have understood. But there's never been one chink in your armour against me, has there? Not one.'

'Never?' he questioned. 'No single occasion? Then don't you remember—or don't you want to remember—a certain night when you let me believe I had drawn you to the very brink of surrender, only for you to throw the ultimate insult in my face? Need I remind you what it was?'

In shame and recall of her remorse, she knew he need not. She had wanted him, ached for him, but rebelling against his arrogant knowledge that he could subdue her, she had taunted him with being merely yet another male to seek her favours that night.

His reaction had terrified her. She had thought it then an extension of the humiliation of her which he had intended. But supposing ... supposing he

had reached his own point of surrender to a desire
which matched hers, where might the aftermath of
their shared release have taken them both in understanding and forgiveness?

She said, 'You were angry about Roland and
Florio Varani. But you weren't just concerned for
—your property? You were able to be jealous?
Jealous of *me*?'

'For love of you, and sick with it. I needed to
claim you ... possess you in the face of any man
who coveted you. That night, if I had taken you in
passion and made you truly my wife—*mine*!—
I'd have forgiven you anything. If I had gone on
blaming you for Jason, I'd have been judging my
own flesh. We were as near as that to the oneness
of marriage—and then you cut across the chance
with the kind of affront no red-blooded man could
take. After that——'

'After that, you never approached me in love
again.'

'Do you think I haven't been tempted?'

'Oh, Zante!' She leaned against him. 'If only I
could be sure I'm not dreaming!'

'Do you want proof that you're not, here and
now?'

'Yes ... *No*.' Fists against his chest, she thrust
back to lean against his encircling arms. 'There's
too much to say—to know. Why did you bring her
—Mrs Coburn—back with you? Were you going to
bring her to Erikona?'

'For her to tell Maria the truth about Jason?
No. I wanted you to know it, and I was going to

send for you to meet us here. But you must see why Maria must never hear it?'

Una nodded slowly. 'Because the truth about him could hurt her more than her belief in his suicide?'

'Because the truth, sordid story that it is, could destroy her, and because I think you have done your work with her only too well, my darling. Too well, that is, for her lasting embitterment over his death. Whatever you have said or done to persuade her to accept it, you have succeeded—or you will.'

'You accused me of over-persuading her that Jason hadn't been victimised,' Una couldn't help reminding him.

'While I was still adamant in my conviction that he had been—and by you, I felt I was being deserted by an ally, and with my scorn for what you had done already undermined by my love, I couldn't afford that,' Zante said.

'But you couldn't admit to loving me? You had to have proof I wasn't guilty before you could?' she asked a little sadly.

'May I be forgiven, my over-inflated family arrogance demanded it. The Diomed honour had to be avenged. Or so I told myself, martyring us all in a cause that never existed, as it turns out. But'— his hands unlinked and slid to her shoulders, holding her off from him—'this you must believe, beloved—if my idea of justice had ever driven you to leave me for some other place, some other life which didn't include me, then the cause would have lost out to you. I couldn't have let you go.'

'I never wanted to go,' she murmured. 'I couldn't

see how you would ever find out you had been wrong about me, but I suppose I've lived on hope from day to day. And if I had ever been tempted to try to leave you, the hold you have had over me through Father would have kept me here.'

Zante nodded. 'Yes, that was brutal, but when the devil drives—— At all costs, I had to keep you by me; see you every day; hear your voice; know that even at the distance I have forced myself to keep you, you were *there*. And you are there for me, aren't you, my Una, my one-girl? Always have been? Always will be? Tell me——?'

But for now she had done with words, and very soon so had he. For a long time they clung together, searching lips and hands and eyes gradually breaking the ice of misunderstanding and reproach and estrangement which had kept them apart.

They were a little apart still, as shy as new young lovers of grasping too much and of yielding too soon. As if they were confident that there was all the time in the world for passion to surge for them, they were content to make this an advance-and-retreat hand-holding session between them; the approach of near-strangers who could hasten slowly, knowing they wouldn't remain strangers for long.

At last Zante said, 'We have to give young Lorna Coburn her dinner.'

'Yes. I'm looking forward to talking to her.'

'And she to you.'

'I shall have to ask her to forgive me for the way I behaved downstairs. When did you mean to send for me to come over to see her?'

'Tomorrow. She will be flying back tomorrow night.'

'You will be staying over to see her off?'

'Not necessarily. After we had seen you, I was going to hand her over to a couple of her girl friends who have been on holiday here and who will be going back to England on the same flight. You and I will be going home.'

'Home.' For the first time the word did not jar on Una's ears. At a sudden thought she asked, 'About your sending for me to meet you here—how do we explain that to Maria and to Father?'

'Easily. They are both so convinced of our idyllic marriage that they will buy it willingly as my understandable impatience to see you again.'

'And now'—at another thought she sighed gratefully—'now Father need never know that it wasn't idyllic from the beginning. What are you doing?' she added as Zante went to the telephone and asked for Reception.

He looked round at her over his shoulder with a grin. 'Having your things brought from wherever they are to here—*if* you've no objection to sharing your husband's room?' he asked.

She dimpled at him. 'None,' she said on a little frisson of excitement.

Two hours later they had dined with Lorna Coburn who, to Una's relief, seemed to have taken no offence at her waspish remarks on their meeting, and was only too anxious to fill in the details of Jason's betrayal and defection.

No, she told Una, she did not know who this other woman was and she had never tried to find out, adding with unexpected charity that if the girl had loved Jason, she must have been cheated and have suffered enough by his death, which had drawn a final line under her affair with him as well as under Lorna's.

Yes, she admitted, she herself had taken a long time to forgive him. But now she knew herself loved by a man who was her all-in-all, Jason no longer troubled her dreams.

When they parted from her at the end of the evening Zante said, 'There goes a happy woman, and the happier for having suffered first.'

Una tucked her arm into his as they walked down the corridor to his suite. 'People don't *have* to be hurt first,' she demurred.

Zante crushed her arm closely to his side. 'Everyone gets hurt at some time or another,' he ruled unanswerably. 'Me, I'd much rather swallow the pill first and be rewarded with the sugar lump later.'

The suite held memories for Una. Surrounded by its luxury, she wondered whether Zante was remembering, as she was, her earlier reaction to his choice of it, and the false intimacy with which it had threatened her. He had been ruthless with her fears. Would he remember his cruel mockery of them and, worse, his complete desertion of her for the night, after rousing her hopes by sharing with her the magic of Athene's temple under the moon?

She stood, hesitant and gauche, willing him to

say something, to make the first move, to understand her shyness of the moment. She knew he was watching her. Waiting and shy too? At last her eyes met his, quizzical, mildly amused. He asked, 'You are not ready?' And then, to the dumb shake of her head, added, 'Shall we go home instead?'

She stared at him. 'Go home? Tonight? How can we? There's no flight as late as this!'

He smiled confidently. 'You belittle the Diomed influence, my darling. If you'd really like to go and will pack for both of us, I'll go and lay about me with my magic wand, and with luck we'll be in our own bridal chamber not long after midnight.'

Una protested faintly, 'Lorna Coburn—we can't just walk out on her like this!'

'She'll hardly miss us. Her friends are calling for her early, and I'll have the florist send her a posy with a card explaining our moonlight flit. Get to work now. I shan't be long.'

In a surprisingly short time he was back. He had booked out of the hotel, had ordered flowers to greet Lorna with her early coffee, had chartered a private plane and a taxi to call for them in five minutes to take them to the airport.

Breathless but happy, Una shook her head at him. 'Zante Diomed, you're crazy!' she accused him.

'I feel crazy,' he said, and tipped the page who came for their luggage outrageously.

But in the foyer there was a hitch. Their bags were already loaded on to the taxi when the desk clerk stopped them.

'A telephone call for Madame,' he said. 'Booth

number two, Madame. Your caller is holding on.'

They went to the booth. Una signalled to Zante 'Father—' and listened, while Zante chafed impatiently, hearing only her side of the conversation, her receptive 'Yes?', her greeting of Daniel, her low 'no—!' of surprise at what Daniel was telling her, and very little more until she said goodbye to him and hung up.

Zante hustled her out to the taxi. 'That was a long call,' he commented. 'What did he want? Maria isn't ill? What was it all about?'

By the street lights which dappled the dark interior of the taxi she watched a little fearfully for his expression as she said, 'It was about Selene.'

'Selene?' he echoed sharply. '*What* about Selene?' Una told him.

He listened, darting clipped questions and comments—Why had no one cabled or telephoned him in London? and—Nonsense to suppose Selene would ever have gone to Florio Varani. And when Una came to the news she had heard from Daniel —Roland Luard? What had *he* to do with Selene? She had never given him a second thought, so far as Zante knew.

Una said tactfully, 'Though it seems he's given more than that to her. I know that once when I said something particularly tart about her, he took her side, and Father says they've seen quite a bit of each other in Corfu. But when he came back from Rhodes and Crete, he told her mother and Maria and Father he'd had no idea she would go off to Italy without saying she'd gone. He had made her promise faithfully she would, and he had believed her.'

'More fool he. He falls for her, lets her persuade him she only needs a chance to become the world's film sweetheart or the screen's *femme fatale*, encourages her to try her luck, and sponsors her to his own relatives in Milan for board and lodging and introductions—and then expects her to pass up an opportunity like that by risking her mother's veto before her leaving home instead of after it!' Zante growled.

'I suppose he trusted her,' Una murmured.

'As well trust a mercurial creature like Selene as try to persuade a butterfly not to alight on a particular flower. Utterly single-minded, Selene, where Selene's interests are concerned. Let's hope for Luard, if he's committed to her, that he can tolerate her tricks. Anyway, the arrangement stands, with Madame Trepano's permission?'

'I hope so. Father said Roland swore, hand on heart, that he had acted for the best, as his Italian uncle has a foot firmly in the film scene and that the family is as strait-laced and square and chaperon-minded as Madame Trepano would wish. Roland won't be there, of course. He has to go back to England to take his B.A. degree. But Selene wants to stay for a year to take drama lessons, and to hope for some screen tests, and apparently her mother has agreed to that.'

'Whereupon I shouldn't be too surprised to hear that Maria and Dorcas decide to set up house together. They have talked of it, but Selene at home has always been Maria's stumbling block,' said Zante.

Una nodded. 'Yes, Maria has said as much to me. Zante——?'

'Yes?'

'Are you—disappointed in Selene? Are you going to miss her very much?'

She had to wait for his answer. When it came— 'For nuisance value and as part of my stock-in-trade, yes,' he said.

'She wasn't a nuisance to you! You admire her. You think she's beautiful!' Una protested.

'And so she is. No special merit in that. Just a happy accident of nature which I daresay she realised in her cradle and has been exploiting ever since. As a model she can throw the perfect pose at the merest hint of suggestion to her. That made her useful to me but not indispensable. And "nuisance" I stand by, for her utter absorption in herself and her exaggerated notion of her own value. A charming, unsnubable, self-obsessed child—no, I shan't miss her too much,' Zante declared.

Una confessed, 'I've been very jealous of her.'

'I've allowed you to be. There have been times when I didn't want to help you.'

She remembered aloud, 'There was the time—on the shore—when I couldn't pose well enough for you to be able to paint me. I knew that Selene could have done, and that you were angry——'

The taxi had stopped. They had reached the car-park of the airport. As Zante helped her out he dropped a kiss upon her hair and whispered, 'Remind me some time to tell you why I couldn't paint you that morning. It's important.'

They had boarded Zante's moored launch in Corfu and had left the lights of the sleeping town behind for the dark sea passage to Erikona. There Zante decided not to rouse the White House for his own car and instead found the local taxi-driver taking a last *ouzo* at the only bar which was still open.

It had been fun, achieving a nefarious entry to their own house without being heard; with their shoes in their hands, they had crept up the stairs; in the darkness of the upper corridor Zante had stubbed his toes on an antique oak chest and had sworn under his breath in Greek; Una had dissolved into helpless giggles which he silenced with three fingers laid on her mouth. At the door of their room at last, he took her shoes from her, set them on the floor with his own, and swept her into his arms on the threshold, over it and into the room before he set her down.

So he *had* known! In his arms she clung to him, her smile tremulous and shy. He said thickly, 'I have waited for too long to do that for my bride,' and with a fingertip touch guided her towards the invitation of the great bed.

Moonlight flooded in from the unshuttered windows, silvering everything it glanced upon and enabling them to see the hungry desire in each other's eyes, though by unspoken agreement they held off the moment of fulfilment, indulging tenderness first, and the sweets of exploration and the murmured half-broken endearments of new lovers.

Zante knelt at the bedside, his arms about her waist, his golden head bent to the caress of her errant fingers.

'Zante——?'

'Yes?' He lifted his head.

'Nothing. Just—"Zante"—like that. Loving your name ... and loving you.'

He caught at her hand and pressed his lips into the crumple of her palm. 'My sweet——'

'Yes?'

'Nothing. Just—"my sweet". And I love you too,' he mimicked her.

'How? Love what about me? And when?'

'From our first meeting. And what? Your smile, your walk, your voice, your compassion——'

'My compassion?'

'For your father. Your courage and your defiance of me. And your body—how I've ached for that! Come——'

He stood and lifted her high and close, his spread hands moulding her yielding softness to his hard muscularity. Then he held her off and, fumbling a little, plucked tentatively as the fastenings which hid her body from him.

She helped him, smiling. Slowly, revealingly, he unwrapped her as if she were a precious, fragile parcel. But when passion stormed him into taking her, she was no inanimate, no mere bundle. She was all there for him; all vibrant woman, as desirous and desiring as he. She flowered in the sweet ecstasy of answering his demands of her, making her own of him. Passion totally shared and spent at last, they lay apart, but still were one.

At last Una said, 'You promised to tell me why you couldn't use me as a model for your painting of Archon. Why you had said your thinking you could had been a mistake.'

'And so it was.'

'Why was it? How did I disappoint you?'

'By being you—mine and not mine, real and warm-blooded—utterly and pulsingly alive. I tried, but I couldn't make you merely one-dimensional on canvas. Feeling for you as I did, it was impossible. My flesh craved yours too much, and there was no way I could turn it into a few brush-strokes simply to create an effect.'

Una sighed happily. 'I thought you were angry because I wasn't Selene. I felt I'd failed you, and I was hurt when you wouldn't tell me what you did want of me.'

He turned towards her again. 'I was wanting then what I've always wanted, but have been too wrong-headed to ask of you. But now you do know what it is?'

Her answer to that was a new claiming of him, a new abandonment to him that was more eloquent than any words.

The **HARLEQUIN CLASSIC LIBRARY** is offering some of the best in romance fiction—great old classics from our early publishing lists.

On the following page is a coupon with which you may order any or all of these titles. If you order all nine, you will receive a free book—*Meet the Warrens*, a heartwarming classic romance by Lucy Agnes Hancock.

The first nine novels in the

HARLEQUIN CLASSIC LIBRARY

Great old favorites...
Harlequin Classic Library
Complete and mail this coupon today!

Harlequin Reader Service

In U.S.A.
MPO Box 707
Niagara Falls, N.Y. 14302

In Canada
649 Ontario St.
Stratford, Ontario, N5A 6W2

Please send me the following novels from the Harlequin Classic Library.
I am enclosing my check or money order for $1.25 for each novel ordered,
plus 59¢ to cover postage and handling. If I order all nine titles, I will receive
a free book, *Meet the Warrens,* by Lucy Agnes Hancock.

☐ 1   ☐ 4   ☐ 7
☐ 2   ☐ 5   ☐ 8
☐ 3   ☐ 6   ☐ 9

Number of novels checked @ $1.25 each = $ _____

N.Y. State residents add appropriate sales tax $ _____

Postage and handling $ _____.59

                                        TOTAL $ _____

I enclose _____
(Please send check or money order. We cannot be responsible for cash sent
through the mail.)
Prices subject to change without notice.

Name _____
            (Please Print)

Address _____

City _____

State/Prov. _____

Zip/Postal Code _____

Offer expires December 31, 1980.   0075633